Seven, thirty-five...
more or less

the search for forgiveness in the afterlife

Steven G. Percifield
© 2016

Introduction

To those who read this, it will come as no shock that I am no longer of the Earth at the time of publishing. Many books have been published posthumously. It might be somewhat more confounding to you, however, to know that this was also the case during the *writing*.

This is not nearly as remarkable as it might seem, as you will come to understand. What *is* remarkable is the fact that this has not occurred countless times before. I have dwelled upon this anomaly without resolution. Perhaps it is because others on the far (from readers' and writers') sides of the divide simply felt no reason to communicate across it. Of those very few who did feel such a desire, having no material form made the taking of "pen in hand" a very difficult option for them. They were relegated to appearing to the living, on very rare circumstances, as an apparition—usually at night, when minds are most receptive. Having no physical form, writing a novel was simply out of the question; how could one pick up a pen or depress a keyboard key? And persuading living beings to set another soul's thoughts to paper involves such metaphysical gymnastics as to totally obfuscate intended words before they could be memorialized.

On the other hand, the transcription of our *own* thoughts from our post-mortem selves to our pre-mortem self, is a fairly straightforward process: As our beings' pre- and post-mortem consciousnesses operate on similar "frequencies," little (if any) need be lost in translation. All that is required is for one's eternal spirit to move from one-fold of time to another, in order to inspire one's still-mortal self.

Although this could have (and probably has) been done previously, I suspect that the rarity of the necessary post/pre-mortem inter-self-communication, compounded by the rarity of those humans with the time to cipher a long, involved message, have combined to minimize (or maybe even prevent) such occurrences. During the writing, being as I was "in between jobs," this problem for me was resolved. Also (and to their eternal credit) most souls—of this world and beyond—have other things, vastly more important to do with their time. For me, on the other hand, time (whatever it is) was all I had, for reasons I hope you will come to understand.

I was fortunate enough to find the way to communicate with my pre-mortem self almost by accident. Once it was done, though, the flow of the words herein was quite easy.

The marvelous thing about writing from the other side is the sheer volume of the material available, unconstrained, as it were, by limited perspective or "natural law," whatever in the world *that* might be.

S. G. P.

Chapter 1

SLAVEMASTER

Securely wrapped in his self-imposed cocoon of darkness aided by the moonless night, dark rage guided him as, with headlights off, he drove slowly through the condominium parking lot, illuminated poorly and partially by the sole sodium lamp near the entrance. The hate grew within him to the exclusion of any other emotion, blocking his rational thought like an eclipsing moon blocks the sun. Any love he had ever known was peripheral to the darkness: a corona, a small glimmer of light, barely surrounding the utter blackness.

His mission was clear…to him at least. To others, less affected by the goings-on of the past two years, what he planned was unthinkably sick. That was only because they didn't understand it from *his* perspective, he told himself. Let them walk a mile in his shoes. Then they would understand.

The early winter dark of Central Indiana had been crisp and cool. Clear skies had allowed yesterday's accumulated warmth to escape from the earth's lower atmosphere. There had been a thick layer of frost on the windshield when he'd first walked out into the driveway, but it had come off easily with just the wipers and a couple of jabs at the windshield washer button. This was a good thing, Billy thought to himself; if he had to wait for the car to warm up to get the defroster going, he might be late. His other option—standing, exposed to curious eyes while scraping the windshield—would have been foolhardy and time consuming. And time was everything. Well, not quite everything; the noise might alert a witness whose testimony he would not welcome if worse came to worse.

He could not be delayed. Every tick of his watch was a potential threat to his planned repossession. His timing had to be near perfect if it were to succeed.

Headlights on in the semi-darkness, he drove the near-empty streets of Carmel, an affluent suburb north of Indianapolis, at a consistent five miles per hour over the posted speed limit. No self-respecting cop would stop him for a 5 mile per hour infraction but driving at or below the limit might call attention to him. Moving east on 146th Street, he came to a 4-way stop at River Road at the same time as a car approaching from the left. Courteous by nature, he waved the car to go on through; besides, it would allow the other driver less chance to see his face. At Noblesville, he turned right onto State Road 32, then left onto State Road 19, following the course of the river before straightening due north to Cicero, Indiana, his destination.

He had rehearsed this task twice, driving this route to the small town of Cicero, at the same early morning time, on the same day of the week. He had practiced well: a 12 to 14-minute drive depending on the stoplights, then 5 minutes of stealth as he waited for *Jerry* to leave. If he arrived too early and someone saw Billy sitting in his car in the dark, they might feel obliged to keep an eye on him. Worse yet, they might call the sheriff or the police. If he arrived just slightly late, Jerry—his estranged father-in-law—might see him enter the lot. And if he arrived *too* long after Jerry left for work, it was likely that neighbors might be up; the sun surely would be. The light, he knew, was his enemy. He chuckled to himself at his thoughts and actions; rather vampiric, he thought. Neighbors would become suspicious if they saw him alone in the parking lot, just sitting there in the gathering light. They might become witnesses. Jerry leaving for his work at the bakery before anyone else was up provided the narrow window of lightless opportunity he needed.

Turning off his headlights, he had entered the town houses' parking lot exactly five minutes before Jerry should be leaving. It wasn't, after all, him with whom he had a quarrel. In any case, he didn't want to confront him. Jerry was built like a bulldozer and would be a threat to his plans—or worse, to his life. It was the two bitches that would remain after Jerry had left that were his objectives. They had stolen from him and he intended to reclaim what was rightfully his.

He drove slowly through the parking lot with his lights off. Headlights would draw attention to anyone coming *into* the parking lot at this early morning hour. On the other hand, he worried the lack of headlamps in the semi-dark would arouse suspicion if anyone did happen to see his moving car. He'd have to count on luck; it had, after all, served him on his many sojourns to Vegas. Driving without headlamps was the lessor of two evils. He continued driving across the condo's parking lot, away from his targets' residence, hoping not to be noticed. He wasn't.

At the end of the lot, between where several boats sat on trailers awaiting next spring's thaw, there was an empty spot. He backed his car in between the boats. From where he sat, the boats would conceal him from most angles. He could look down the length of the parking lot and would see Jerry's car as it departed. But Jerry, looking in the opposite direction would not see him.

For a brief second, he glanced into his rearview mirror and took in the bucolic serenity of the still waters of Morse Reservoir. The waters were calming—too calming, he realized. They calmed him, distracted him. He could not allow that to happen.

He was, he realized, monomaniacal. He had to concentrate on one thing only. In his forty-plus years, he had forced himself not to be the scatter-brained youth he had been accused of being. To accomplish anything required his absolute focus on his intended task, to the exclusion of everything else. When he had met Dawn, only a couple of years before, he knew he must focus on her with laser-beam intensity if she were to be his. She was beautiful, smart and vivacious. He was smitten. Had she been only a few months younger, she would have been jail-bait in Indiana, as he was in his late-30s. But that would not have mattered to him. He had to possess her; he had to add her to his collection.

Over the next year and a half, they maintained an alternating love/hate relationship in which they both found reinforcement—and emancipation from their parents. In short order, like a bold explorer, he claimed her, planting his flag in her virgin soil. A couple of months later, the fecundity of their union was confirmed by a doctor and they were married, establishing his legal claim of her to the rest of the world.

But like colonialists of history, who soon followed the explorers, he soon learned—to his dismay—that adding a possession to his empire and controlling it were two entirely different things.

He physically jerked as he brought himself back to the reality of the moment and his mission. He could not permit his attention to wander again. He turned the car's heater to a hotter setting and moved the fan control to "high" to counteract the cold sweat that was forming all over his body. Like a hawk atop a phone pole overlooking a recently harvested field, he scanned the parking lot to the south, alert for any tell-tale movement. Unmoving, his gaze was fixed in a direction but unfocused on any point. It was movement, not detail, he sought.

And there it was; the movement in the right periphery of his vision set off an alarm in his head. He focused on the undefined movement and recognized Jerry's car sink slightly as Jerry settled into it. Steam from the engine's combustion escaped the tailpipe forming small clouds as the car backed up, turned and proceeded away from him, across the parking lot, and toward the street.

Reaching into the glove compartment, he pulled out a nickel-plated Colt Python. Its .357 magnum rounds were more than sufficient to accomplish his goal. And its relatively short 4" barrel made it easy to conceal. His jacket, still open at the front, he slid the pistol into his right pants pocket, zipping the jacket closed to conceal it. As he swung his feet to the ground and began to stand, he whispered a curse (not too loud, he hoped) as the barrel of the Colt gouged him in the crotch.

 At a brisk pace, he walked south through the parking lot, a nervous shiver running up and down his body. The shiver did not come from the cold. Despite the chill, he was sweating as if in a sauna. The enormity of his chosen task was permeating his body, mind and soul. He turned to the left on a walkway, then one more immediate right which brought him to the town house's front door.

Opening the storm door and stepping between it and the entry door, he removed the pistol from his pants and depressed the door's chime button with the tip of the muzzle, careful to conceal his action with his body. He heard the faint sound of the bell behind the closed door, then stood there for what seemed an eternity. No one came to open the door. He waited, then pressed the chime button again. What the hell was wrong with these people? He knew they were there. He pressed it a third time at the exact moment that the door opened. Somehow, he felt stupidly embarrassed by having rung the chime even as the door opened.

"Billy!" was all Cheryl said as she stood there, a look of shock and surprise on her face. Inadvertently, her gaze dropped to the pistol in his hand. Instinctively, she attempted to block his entrance and close the door. With little effort he pushed the door and Cheryl out of his way and stepped inside, kicking the door shut behind him with his heel, never taking his eyes off hers. He didn't remember exactly what she had said to him or when; she muttered something about God. He only recalled shoving the barrel of the Colt into her midsection, wishing her a Merry Christmas, and pulling the trigger. She fell to the floor like a rag doll, but her mouth was still going, pleading, begging and at the same time asking God to forgive him. Standing over her, cursing her with every vile word he could form, at nearly point-blank range he pointed the gun at her head and fired a second time, just as Dawn came running at him. Cheryl's movement ceased.

Ignoring Billy completely, Dawn ran towards her fallen mother. The third shot from Billy's pistol, though, dropped her in her tracks. She crumpled to the floor just inches from her mother's glazing eyes. But she failed to die from Billy's first shot. She lay there trying to speak but only making mewing, cat-like sounds.

Billy put the muzzle of his gun against her temple and fired again ensuring she would go no further in her rebellion against him. He ran up the stairs, grabbed his infant son, wrapped him in a blanket and carried him carefully back to his car. Placing the infant prone upon the front seat, he wrapped a seatbelt around him and clicked it shut. He did not have a child safety seat and did not want to risk injury to the child if he had to brake hard. He talked calmly to the baby as he deliberately drove away at the posted speed limit...plus five miles per hour.

Chapter 2—

TWENTY-THREE YEARS LATER

Eerily quiet. Faint shadows almost—but not quite—distinguishable on the bedroom walls. Pre-dawn light beginning to filter through suspended particles of frozen snow hanging in the dark, dank winter air of Chicagoland.

Sleep had been an elusive goal as I had tossed and turned for nights on end fighting the ravages of a flu that had become pneumonia. But during *this* night's restless sleep, the aches, pains, and coughing fits which had worn me down were now, thankfully, subsided. I gave a silent prayer of gratitude for the end to my suffering.

I hated to awaken her; she had worn herself down, ministering to me day and night for the last six weeks. But now it appeared that her care and concern had worked; I felt no discomfort. I wanted to share this great news with her. I rolled over, closer to her. As usual, she was laying on her left side, her back to me. Slowly, so as not to startle her, I reached out with my left hand, gently placing it onto the gentle curve of her right hip, and attempted to rock her.

"Sue," I said, "it's gone; the pain I mean. I feel better. You did it. You're a regular Clara Barton."

She did not stir. She did not respond in any way to my light-hearted attempt to humorously awaken her. Should I let her sleep? She was like a burned-out light bulb; she had been "on" for so many hours it was as if her filament had finally burned through. As much as I wanted to share my good news with her, it would be selfish for me to deprive her of the rest she needed…and deserved. I glanced up at the clock on the dresser. In the dim pre-dawn light, I could barely make out the positions of its black hands, dark shadows against an unlighted white background. I strained my eyes.

It was 7:35…more or less.

———————————————

I would let her sleep. I would get up and walk around the house, savoring the freedom of being able to do so without being racked by the pain within my ribcage.

As usual, the cat—Biscut—was on top of the covers, in between my feet. I don't really like cats (or so Sue says I say). I am a dog person; a completely different relationship, Cats are like the squirrels in the trees; cute, warm-blooded, fuzzy and independent. Dogs are like immediate family; like kids: dependent, reactive, sometimes naughty, but loved and loving. But the little fur-ball *is* kind of cute…and he *does* interact with me… at least in a "cat" sort of way. In fact, at seventeen years of age, she's been with us one and a half times as long as my beloved yellow lab, Buddy, God rest his soul.

I chuckled as I considered the sign I had passed, at a tiny crossroads village out in the country as I drove through St. John near the Illinois-Indiana border a few months before. At the village's one intersection, a Methodist church sat on one side, a Catholic church opposite it. It was the week of the Catholic church's annual blessing of the pets. On the church's marquis, was the message, "All dogs go to heaven." The rector (I assumed) was walking away from the marquis, having just posted the message. The Methodist marquis had the message, "Chili for charity dinner, Sunday—6:00 PM." I drove on. Upon my return that evening, the marquis at the Methodist church had been changed to read, "Dogs do not have souls."

I couldn't see her with the bedspread pulled up to my chin, but I knew Chloe was there. If I moved gently, I hoped not to disturb her. Retracting my knees to my chest, I rotated my feet to the edge of the bed and dropped them to floor. Sitting now, I could see her. She was in place, exactly where she always was when I awoke, but she was not asleep. He sat unmoving, eyes wide open, staring at where I had just laid. Cats have a spooky way of staring at something, oblivious to everything else around them, focused without interacting. I'd often wondered whether their natural behavior was linked to some form of "autism by design;" perhaps God had engineered them that way to help them hunt, oblivious to all but movement.

I congratulated myself on the gentle discretion of my own movement. Even the bedspread, under which my legs had rested, was unmoved, still arching over the tunnels left in the blankets where my legs had been.

Moving carefully in the semi-dark I walked to the restroom and stopped at the toilet. It was my ritual upon getting up. Hell; at my advancing age, it had become my ritual three times a night *and* when I finally got up for good. But today, for some reason, I didn't need to go. Perhaps because of all the meds I had been taking. Ah, to be young again.

Oh, well; I was up. I might as well stay up. I passed through the bath, to the laundry and turned into the kitchen, going to the window over the kitchen sink. Looking out, I was surprised to see at least six inches of just fallen and totally unpredicted snow. It must be cold out. But in our snug little house, I did not feel it.

I thought of brewing some coffee but decided against it; it had none of the appeal it normally exerted upon me in the early morning. *The meds again,* I wondered? Instead, I drifted through the living room and sat upon the sofa. Looking out over the front lawn, the streetlights glinted off the snow particles hanging in the air, creating countless tiny pinpoints of light.

It fascinated me that something as mundane as winter snow in Chicagoland could exhibit such beauty. I sat there watching for what seemed to me to be the better part of an hour, even though—as far as I could tell in the gloom—the sun had risen no further. The cloud cover and airborne snow must be stifling the light. Restless, after so many days in bed, I walked up the bedroom hallway and into the room where my stepson had resided following his separation from his job and, shortly thereafter, his family. I stood there wondering how someone like him—a truly good person, supremely talented, hardworking, and so dedicated to his family—could have it all come apart. I smiled to myself knowing that being a good person, and being as talented as he was, he would find a way of creating a new, wonderful life, even if different from the one he had known. I had prayed that, eventually, he and his children would get back together. The breakup of his family had been a blow to all concerned. What had bothered me most, though, was that when he and his wife separated, his wife and daughters had separated from my wife and me as well. Sue had been shattered by her grandchildren's estrangements from her. She sent them holiday cards, birthday cards, and presents without reply. Her heart was broken but she had kept it all inside of her, saving her emotional energy for the son who, she knew, needed it even more.

I walked into the third bedroom, my office, a mess just as I'd left it on the last day I'd been able to work. A half-eaten box of sourdough pretzels sat on my desk, crumbs strewn about the desk-top and my office chair. Once, long ago, I had cleaned my office but could find nothing after having done so. I did not make that mistake again. Any further cleaning was done for purely hygienic reasons. I chuckled to myself; it was better that way, I rationalized. What was it the wall plaque of my mother-in-law (God rest *her* soul) had said? *Clean enough to be healthy—dirty enough to be happy.*

I sat at my chair, in front of my cluttered desk, looking out the window at the huge hard-maple tree, dormant beside the driveway in back. The tree swing we had put up for our grandchildren hung unmoving from a massive, barren horizontal limb; snow at least eight inches deep had settled atop the swing's wooden seat, the bottom of which was barely inches above the deep snow on the ground. The swing had been hung with love in anticipation of the times our grandchildren—both Sue's and mine—would spend upon it. In the years we had lived there, it had been used only twice. I noted that the squirrels had chewed on the ropes that suspended the seat; the fraying of the lines was visible from fifty feet away. Damn squirrels. I would need to climb up there and inspect the rope; maybe replace it. God forbid that the little ones be harmed; although they weren't so little now. I so looked forward to the warmth of spring when the canopy of thick, beautiful green leaves would shade the swing and all that was within forty feet of the trunk.

I stood and walked back to our bedroom. The cat was still in the same spot, still staring toward where I had lain. Sue, too, was where I had left her. I walked to her bedside and again placed my hand on her hip. "Honey," I said, gently pushing back and forth to rock her, "please wake up. I've got some great news; I feel great." She did not respond. With more force, I moved my arm back and forth, attempting to rock her harder. "Honey, wake up!" I was becoming frantic. She was three years older than me and, back before a woman was "supposed" to have them, had sustained a massive, near-fatal heart attack. "Please honey, wake up!" Nearly panicked, I was trying to rock her with all my might. Despite my efforts she lay there unmoving.

"Oh, God no," I pleaded! "Please, don't let her be gone."

As if struck by a bolt of lightning, I jerked upright contemplating the possible horror of my being alone when it hit me. I looked over the scene before me: My wife, unmoving on the bed; the cat still sitting atop the blankets, still staring at the same spot. The snow seemingly hanging in the air, did not just *seem* to hang, it truly was unmoving. In the nightmare of my reality, I turned to look at the rest of the room. I saw the clock atop the dresser.

It was still 7:35…more or less, even after all that had occurred.

Chapter 3

DISEMBARKATION

Surely, I was losing my mind. How grossly unfair, I thought to myself. First I nearly lose my life to pneumonia. Between two bouts with unrelated life-threatening diseases and a near-fatal car accident, it was the third time in seven years that I had been on death's doorstep. Now, having survived all of these, I am feeling no pain but am obviously going insane.

I nearly ran to the bathroom and stood before the sink, gazing into the mirror above it. But no one looked back. No one. Instead, as I looked at the mirror in front of me, I saw behind me only partially illuminated formless grey shapes beyond the open door to the laundry room. "Sue!" I screamed. Somehow, I didn't expect a reply. None came.

Returning to the bedroom, I returned to the bedside of my wife's prone form and, once again, with all my strength, attempted to rock her to consciousness. My arms moved back and forth like a lumberjack's working a 2-man saw. But Sue did not move, not even an inch.

Curious, I thought to myself, *and terrifying.*

I turned to the bedroom window behind me, my elbows on the sill and the mass of my bowed head weighing upon my hands. I raised my head and folded my hands. A little fresh air: perhaps that would help. I reached up to the latch on the closed window. My fingers moved. The latch did not. I looked out through the window and it struck me; the pinpoints of light reflecting off of the crystals of falling snow were like particles of silt glinting in the sunlight of a flowing stream…but they truly were not moving. They sat motionless, suspended in the air. My mind whirled as I began to put the bits and pieces of accumulated evidence together. Like one stone after another lain atop a condemned Colonial murderer, the weight of the evidence was slowly, inevitably crushing the life out of me.

My pain was gone. My cough was gone. The cat had not moved, despite the fact that I had gotten up from beneath her. I glanced in her direction anew as my mind began adjusting to my dawning realization. Not surprisingly, she still sat in the exact same place, in the same position, staring sphinxlike up the bed to where I had been.

I followed her gaze. There, beneath the covers at the head of the bed, the bedspread drawn up to my chin was…

Me.

Unmoving.

Panicked, seeking anything rational in what had become my irrational universe, I looked about the room and saw the calendar on the dresser. It was Sunday January 20. I glanced again at the clock atop the chest of drawers on Sue's side of the bed.

It was still 7:35; the official time of my death according to the death certificate someone would issue at some later time.

Whatever time is.

Like a hurtling freight train impacting a car stuck on a railroad crossing, the lot of my new situation struck, annihilating everything before it. Recognizing the futility of trying to change my newly realized circumstance, realizing that I had crossed to the other side, curious as to the limitations death had imposed upon me or removed from me (even though I could not yet fully accept my death as such), I wandered back through the kitchen and out to the living room where I again sat on the couch, morose, gazing out at the beauty of the falling—no, not falling—gazing out at the beauty of the snow crystals suspended—apparently for eternity—in the air.

Was I really dead? Had time really stopped? I had to be. *It* had to have. Was this hell? Was this to be my lot forever; alone, through eternity, in a world in which I could not play a part? Upon which I could have no effect? Surrounded by inanimate objects and people with which I could not interact? I pondered such an existence and decided it was assuredly not what I wanted. It was not even something I could tolerate. Was it even something I could stoically endure? No. Surely, it was not. Yet what alternative did I have if I could not endure it? I couldn't even take my life.

It was already taken.

Chapter 4

THE STATION MASTER

Had I the need—or, for that matter, the ability—to do so, I would have peed my pants, the voice startled me so. For hours (it seemed, but who could really tell), I had not heard a sound nor had I witnessed movement of any kind. And then, without warning, the voice:

"Son," it said in a voice I knew and loved, "I've missed being with you." My father, dead over ten years, walked up to where I was sitting. Although he wasn't the frail, almost 90-year old man I too had missed. He was a younger, robust man in his mid or late forties. He was carrying a golf bag. What a strange thing to be carrying, I thought, in the dead of winter (no pun intended). He sat it down. I looked about me; I was no longer in our house in Joliet, IL. We were in the house in which I'd grown up in Indianapolis.

I was seated on an overstuffed chair, at one side of the living room's large picture window. Dad sat opposite me, on the couch, facing the window. Bright sunlight, brighter than any I had experienced before, flooded the room. The grass, shrubs and leaves outside were all a vivid, verdant green, the color of late spring.

"Is this what I think it is," I asked? "Am I dead?"

"You figured it out quicker than I did," Dad replied, a twinkle in his eye, "but just in the physical sense. As you'll learn, dead is not the right word. You're just in your new, uh...dimension I guess would be the right word."

"It's not what I imagined," I said, flatly.

"What did you imagine?"

"You know, like what I was taught in Sunday school when I was a kid; clouds, wings, harps, angels...all that stuff."

Dad chuckled. "That's what some find. Maybe you will too if that is what you're looking for. Your journey isn't over. It's just beginning. Seek and ye shall find," he said, quoting the scriptures as he often did late in his life.

I stood from the chair; Dad stood from the couch. We walked toward one another and embraced. "I can't tell you how much I've missed you since you left," I said.

"I never left. In fact, I've always been here. It's just so great talking with you again. I always loved talking with you...well, almost always." Dad winked at me. We both knew of the many times of my youth to which he referred.

Standing in front of him, I looked down at my feet. The same posture I had taken in front of him during my high school days when I had to explain where I had been or what I had been up to, the strange smell of my breath, or why I didn't want him to go out to the garage. I laughed at the return of a long-repressed memories.

"Is Mom here?" I asked. She had died nearly ten years before my father after a long, excruciating (for them both) battle with cancer.

"Everything is here," Dad replied. "All you have to do is look for it."

"How do I do that?"

"Like I said, you just have to seek it."

I raised my eyes to ask him another question; "How?"

He was gone. I was alone again.

I found myself crying.

But no tears came.

Just emptiness. Then nothing.

Chapter 5

THE BEGINNING OF THE PATH

Terror gripped me. How long I had been here I had no way of knowing. There was nothing around me, no scale of anything against which to measure; I was in a void—not dark, but not light either. I looked down at my hands. I didn't see them; there was nothing there. No hands, nothing behind where they should have been. Just…nothing; no sights, no sounds, and no feelings: just complete, absolute sensory deprivation.

I had, it seemed, only my thoughts and even these were ephemeral sparks with no substance. The most outstanding of these were the most recent: my conversation with my dad. What had he meant; all I had to do was look for it? How could I look? There was nothing here to look *AT*. Could I possibly go somewhere else? Could I miraculously teleport over miles; over light years of distance; over centuries of time? How did *he* find *me*? How could he know where I was? How had he come to be with me? Could *he* go anywhere *he* desired? Be any*thing*?

Could *I* go anywhere *I* desired; be anything; at any time I chose?

My nonsensical thought fragments cleaved to one another beginning to coalesce into rudimentary patterns of logic. They drifted back to my childhood home in Indianapolis: the house where I'd lived (excepting college) from grade school until my first marriage, the house where I had just met with my father. It was such a wonderful house. My grandfather—my mom's dad—had built it. He had designed it with my mom and drawn up the plans. Meticulous to the point of mania, he had hand-selected each and every piece of wood, every load of stone. Grandpa pre-qualified and hired every sub-contractor; he micro-managed them to the point of physical conflict. That was his nature. No one ever questioned where they stood with him. He was only too happy to tell them, whether they liked it or not. He and my dad had done most of the framing carpentry on the house. He nearly drove my dad as nuts as he had the subs. Nevertheless, they all respected him. And my dad loved him like the father he had had only occasionally.

His own father was a wonderful person…when he wasn't drinking. But that wasn't often. Fiercely independent, smart and ambitious, he was a "tinner"—a sheet metal and furnace man—by trade. At various times he had been a lawman, a carnival trick-shot artist, a farmer and had operated—with my paternal grandmother—a mobile kitchen following the lumber camps through Wisconsin and Minnesota. His spirit had diminished over time as it became clear to him that he would never achieve the lofty goals he had established for himself. He sought to replace his diminished spirits with store-bought ones. As time passed, this replacement became nearly complete. Most regrettably, while alcohol helped him overcome the pains of life, it also inflamed him against other people. On a regular basis, his drunken rages left his wife, two daughters and one son terrified of him…and for good reason. Drinking and fighting diminished him—spiritually and physically. He had left one eyeball and a part of one ear on a sawdust-covered tavern floor in Franklin, Indiana. His bad habits, of which smoking was the least, took his life at a fairly early age.

Even before that, however, my maternal grandfather had become like a stepfather to my dad.

I walked around the west end of the house marveling at how modern it had seemed in my youth and how dated now: Indiana limestone at the bottom, pink "Florida stone" from the windowsills up to the wide eaves and aluminum framed windows—energy was not a concern or a significant cost factor back then. I walked to the back yard and gazed out at the vacant field behind it. A deep ravine, cut it in two, caused by the occasional stream following a rain. The topography made the field un-buildable, providing a perfect place for the adventures of a growing boy. Weather permitting, I had nearly lived in that field hunting snakes and toads, building forts with my friends, playing, fighting, and sometime just sitting in the sun laying back on a bed of Queen Anne's Lace crushed beneath me, looking at the sky and doing nothing (except becoming infested with chiggers—I hated them; they always attacked the most secluded and sensitive parts of the body).

Turning, I walked toward the house's back stoop where my pigeon (I had rescued it as a nestling) roosted atop the back-porch light fixture. Rescuing it had been the least I could do after having thrown a rock which knocked the squab from its nest under the eaves of the Morgan Canning Factory in Franklin, adjacent to my grandma's house.

The back door to our house opened. Mom, wearing a floral print dress and a bib apron with wide ruffles, walked out, a radiant smile on her face. "I've been expecting you," she said. "Come in and get washed up for lunch."

I ran to her, threw my arms around her, and hugged her. She, just like my dad, appeared to be in her mid-forties. "Mom," I said, choking back tears, "I'm so glad I found you. There is so much I want to ask you."

"I know. Now get in there and wash your hands. I didn't know you were coming so I didn't have time to prepare much. I hope PBJs are OK. I made them just the way you like them: butter, chunky peanut butter and strawberry jam. Oh, and be sure to drink your milk."

I headed to the half-bath at the end of the family room, washed up and returned to the breakfast table. Mom was already sitting but politely, as always, waited until both of us were seated before touching her food.

Ravenously, I tore into my sandwich which I found curious as I felt no hunger; force of habit I told myself. "Don't take such big bites." I started to take another bite and then, remembering her words, picked up the glass of milk she had placed before me, and took a deep drink. It was cool and clean tasting and perfectly complemented my sandwich. Mom smiled.

I quickly finished my lunch. I had so much to talk about, so many questions. Mom was one of the smartest people I would ever know. She should have been the valedictorian of her very large high school class at Arsenal Technical. She had the best grades among her classmates. But back then, having a girl for valedictorian just *wasn't done*. So, she sat on the stage as salutatorian, as a boy with lesser grades gave the commencement speech. In any case, I knew she would have the answers.

"Mom," I began, "there is so much that happened after you—uh—died. I want to tell you all about it."

She smiled. "No need, honey. I was there with you every step of the way. I saw everything that happened. I knew your every thought."

I recoiled. "Mom, I'm sorry," I said. I had had so many thoughts that I was ashamed of, even thinking that they were known only to me. The idea that my mother might have known them was both embarrassing and humiliating.

"Honey, don't be bothered. One thing about existing on the human level is that everyone has thoughts, urges and desires, many of them biological in origin, some of which they want to share and some of which they prefer to keep hidden…even from themselves." She smiled again…knowingly. "The thing that separates us from lesser animals, during our time as humans, is that we also have an overwhelming consciousness that is much more than biological in origin. We have a level of consciousness that is a God-given sense of spirituality; it is our souls. It is divine."

I decided to throw her a curve and see how she handled it.

"So how would you describe our current state of existence? How does it compare with our human state? Are we in heaven or hell? Where is God?" I knew she would have answers. None of my friends, even the supposed intellectuals among them, had ever bested her in debates ranging from philosophy to science to religion to differences in politics. She was a rare combination. A pro-Goldwater delegate to the '64 Republican National Convention, she embraced conservative economics, deeply held religious views, was a crack shot, and had been an avid hunter. At the same time she espoused these seemingly *Republican* leanings, she had been a staunch supporter of both the civil rights and women's rights movements, acceptance of anyone and everyone, and a supporter of the ASPCA. She never considered these as paradoxes.

"Let me answer, in no particular order," Mom began. "God is all around us. He is creation. He preceded creation. He *created* creation. He was there when we were inserted into our human bodies and times; he is here now that we've been released from them. Energy, for example," she continued, "is eternal, neither created nor destroyed. God is the sum total of all the energy in the universe and beyond and much more even than that; He preceded energy; He is the sum total of everything; not just the three dimensions we recognized as humans, but *all* dimensions. Our individual consciousness, our thought, is an infinitesimally small portion of that total. But it *is* a vital part of it. Thought is a form of energy. Though it can't be destroyed, energy can change form. In your present form, your thought energy has survived beyond your physical body. You are like pure *thought* energy. You can be one with God, as a part of his total, which he recognizes as such. To that degree, all humans are divine. As to how our present state compares to our human existence (she paused for effect) it doesn't.

As humans," she continued, "our conscious energy—our thoughts—took the form of electro-chemical processes in our brains. With the death of our bodies, that energy was released but continues to exist in a different, purer, higher form as a small part of the total. The total is God. In human forms, we can't really conceive of this. So, people invented allegories—understandable to the limited human mind—to try to explain it. These allegories are the basis of *all* worldly religions; they all seek to understand and explain our relationship to God, our relationship to creation, which (she laughed) is everything we *can't* even comprehend. In essence, all religions try to explain just three things: where did we come from, what are we doing here, and where are we going?"

I sat, trying to absorb her explanation but it raised more questions than it answered.

She continued: "As humans, we attempt to dichotomize everything: God versus Satan, good versus bad, Republican versus Democrat, Ford versus Chevy." She laughed again; we were Chevy people—or had been until I bought 3 new lemons in a row. "It's easier for humans to think that way. Heaven or Hell, though, are not the black or white, cut and dried polar opposites that our human minds can grasp. There are infinite shades of grey between. More than that: there are infinite shades beyond the blackest black or whitest white, beyond even the highest reaches of heaven and the lowest depths of hell. Our human existences were merely a different state of being in which the good or evil that is a part of each of our metaphysical beings was displayed...sometimes to others more than ourselves. Only one person in the human state was pure good. However, you *do* reap what you sew. Those whose energy was largely devoted to "good" are closer to (and a larger part of) the infinite total that is God; those whose energies were not so well devoted, are further from—and a smaller part of—Him. They exist on the periphery of everything else, removed from it, and existing alone in a void."

"Is the void Hell?" I asked, concerned about my own experience within it. Strangely—and perhaps significantly—she ignored my question and went on.

"God, the sum total, is the center of all that is, matter and non-matter, with the light of a trillion suns and is the total of all that is. Good," she went on, "is of a higher order than evil and therefore is possessed of more energy. If one's consciousness is largely good, one possesses more God-like energy and is therefore a larger part of—and nearer to—Him. That is why truth, justice and all that is good eventually triumph—overall, but not in *every* situation." I noted, with a mixture of amusement and curiosity, her use of the male pronoun in reference to God, trying to reconcile it with her feminist views. Apparently reading my thoughts, she said, "In the word of Captain James T. Kirk, male and female are universal constants."

I sat, pondering my mother's explanation, trying to understand it, trying to think of ways to challenge her explanation. I had it. "Even a rock possesses some energy. Are you suggesting that a rock is one with God the same way we are?"

"Yes," she replied without pause, "just as all of creation is; but on such an infinitesimally lesser level as to make comparison useless. The difference between the energy levels of inanimate objects like a rock and a living thing such as a plant, is like the distance from one end of the house to the other; from a plant to a dog, the difference is like the distance from Earth to the moon; Between a dog and a human it's like the distance from the Earth to the sun; between an Earth-bound human and us as we now are, it's like light years to the nearest solar system.

And from us to God it's greater than the distance from Earth to the farthest fringes of the universe."

"Do all living things have an afterlife?"

Mom smiled: "Didn't you say energy is neither created nor destroyed."

"So Buddy is here?" Buddy, a large, lean stray yellow Labrador retriever had been my best friend and life support following the break-up of my first marriage.

"Yes dear. Everything is here. Let me ask you a question: when you were out back by the field looking at the Queen Anne's lace and the fox weed, were they real?"

"I think so. They seemed that way."

"They were. What you saw was the revitalized energy of what they had also been on Earth, in the form you sought and with which you were familiar."

"So Buddy is here, too? In the same form?"

"Yes...if that is what you seek."

"How do I find him?"

"Remember what your father said: seek and ye shall find."

For some reason, I wanted to avert her gaze. I looked down at the crumbs left on the empty plate in front of me. I wasn't sure why I felt I couldn't look at her. Perhaps it was the shame at realizing that she had known the thoughts, my perversions, which I thought I had kept hidden—from the rest of the world, from her, even from myself. Perhaps she knew, even now, what I was thinking.

I looked up at my Mom.

She was no longer there.

Nothing was.

Except the void.

Silently, I screamed. It *was* Hell. The void was hell.

Then I comforted myself as much as possible with soothing recollections of Buddy.

Chapter 6

FUZZY YELLOW BALL

I looked about me unsure of how I'd gotten there.

I was standing on the cracked asphalt at the edge of the parking lot of the condo I had rented after my first wife's and my separation in Naperville, IL. From where I stood, an empty field—a flood plain actually—stretched 150 yards, gently sloping down to the bank of the calmly flowing Du Page River.

It was mid-summer, very early morning. The prairie grasses in the field were thick and nearly chest high even this early in their growing season. Their stems and leaves were calming greens, their blossoms exciting red, yellow and blue pastels. The wildflowers screamed their colors at me, a building crescendo in the increasing sunlight. The morning dew was clinging to them. The dew reflected the rising sun's rays like millions of glistening, tiny, multi-colored stars. The fragrances of the flowers hung over the field, slowly drifting with the thinning remnants of the disbursing mists of the river valley.

I could detect movement in the tall grasses, as the tops of some of them moved without syncopation with the gentle warm breeze wafting from the south. Whatever was moving in the grass was large and moving toward me...rapidly. I was not the least bit afraid, though. I had, after all, been in this position many times. I observed the tell-tale wave of the grass tops moving toward me in a straight line except for an occasional dodge to the left or right. Whatever it was, it was almost upon me. It was then that I saw the tell-tale tail tip, just inches above the tops of the flora.

Buddy burst from the wall of grasses and ran straight at me at full gallop, a fresh, yellow tennis ball, covered in saliva, in his mouth. Stopping just before bowling me over, he stopped at my feet, turning in three tight circles within the length of his body. After his final revolution, he sat down on his haunches, tennis ball still in mouth, looked up at me briefly, lowered his head and dropped the ball at my feet. He looked up again into my eyes as if to say, *c'mon boss, you know the drill, throw it.*

Bending over I picked up the slippery ball. Years of playing baseball and then softball had left me with what was still a pretty good arm. I heaved the ball most of the way to the stream where it disappeared into the tall weeds. Even before the ball had left my hand, Buddy plunged back into the weeds. I tracked his movement by the tops of the moving grasses. For nearly 50 yards, he ran in a straight line following the trajectory of my throw. He then slowed down and began working side-to-side, following his nose, continuing toward the river. His sideways deviations from his course were at first three or four feet each way, then five or six, then ten or twenty. Then they narrowed again very rapidly from twenty feet, to ten feet, to five feet, to none. The movement in the grass stopped. The ripple in the grass tops was now moving back towards me in a straight line.

Again, Buddy burst from the weeds with the ball in his mouth. Again, he did his circular dance in front of me, looked up into my eyes, dropped the ball at my feet and again looked up in anticipation of my next throw. We repeated this scenario perhaps five more times before, after returning to me with ball in mouth, rather than his circular dance and a ball dropped at my feet, he sat on his haunches, ball still in his mouth and just looked at me.

We knew, both of us, what he wanted.

"Go on," I said and waved my arm out across the field. With no hesitation he jumped up, making a beeline through the tall grass, tennis ball still in mouth. In an unwavering line, he headed for the riverbank 150 yards away. Over the muffled din of light nearby traffic, I heard a plaintive "splash."

Oblivious to brambles tearing at my jeans, I pushed my way through the prairie grasses to the river's edge. Exiting the weeds between a stately old sycamore tree and a weeping willow, I stood on the bare bank and watched as Buddy cavorted in the water of the stream, running, and splashing through the low spots, swimming in the deep ones, cooling off. His Yellow Labrador genes were clearly evidenced by his retriever instincts; the tennis ball was held firmly in his mouth, but never dropped, crushed, or bitten.

From a close yet safe distance, mallards and Canada geese shared the water with Buddy. Although wary of the 90-pound dog, they were unafraid. They had seen it all before, many times and realized they had nothing, really, to fear from this large canine. Finally, cooled off, Buddy waded to the shore, dropped the tennis ball at my feet, shook himself dry (covering me in his dispersed water) and lowered his head to drink from the river. He picked the ball, dropped it at my feet again and turned to look downstream. Just as *I* had been trained by *him*, I picked the ball up and threw it twenty or thirty yards down the middle of the river. Buddy ran out to the deep water, splashing through the shallows, then began swimming with the current as the ball moved steadily south with the water's flow. By the time he caught up with it, he was sixty yards away. In one sideways motion of his snout, he snatched the floating ball into his mouth, turned, then paddled strongly to the shore. He scampered up the steep sides of the creek bank then ran along it, directly back to me.

When he arrived at my feet, he didn't do his circle dance. He didn't drop the ball. He just looked into my eyes and with his. With them, as only a dog could say, he spoke: "Thanks boss. I've had all the exercise I want for now. I'm cooled off by my swim. I'm tired. Let's go home."

I walked back up the path I had made in the weeds. Buddy, ball securely in mouth, followed immediately behind me.

———————————

I feared I might again fall into the void. But a tiny fragment of what I had just experienced with Buddy remained with me, growing into random thought droplets which precipitated a memory.

I recalled an intersection in a town near where I lived. Catholic and Baptist churches sat upon opposite corners. One day, while alive, I was driving through the intersection in the late spring. The date coincided with the Catholic Church's "blessing of the pets" at which parish members brought their pets to the church yard to receive a blessing from the priest. I noticed the church marquee's message: "All dogs go to heaven."

I chuckled to myself as I drove on. What a sweet thought.

Two days later, driving through the same intersection, I couldn't help but notice the marquee of the Baptist church across the street: "Animals," it said, "do not have souls."

I had laughed aloud at these dueling theologies.

From first-hand experience, I'm here to say that dogs *do* have souls; even if they are infinitely less than those of humans, they are infinitely more than anything else.

I think. At very least, it's what I choose to believe.

Again, I sat at the breakfast table with Mom. I was dumbfounded by the fact that I had returned to her presence. "I...uh...I...was just with Buddy," I stammered.

"I know."

"But how?"

"How do I know or how were you with him?"

"How was I with him?"

"Spiritual recollection," Mom answered. "Spirit includes the sum total of all you've ever experienced or will experience. It includes everything from your physical life, from before it and after it."

"I don't recall anything before it."

"You will. The spirit evolves just as your physical body did. The closer your spirit moves toward God, the more you will understand. Of course, if your spirit moves away from Him, you will understand less and your recollections will be primarily those of your physical existence. Among those in the physical realm, it's thought of as past-life experiences. Sometimes, those with highly developed spirituality link their previous existence with their new one and encounter vivid spiritual recollections of what went before."

I found my head swimming as I tried to grasp the significance of everything my mother had just explained. More so, I tried to grasp what this meant to me; what did my inability to recall anything other than my physical life and those things I was now experiencing say regarding the position of my soul relative to God?

And yet, even as I contemplated these mysteries, I found my cognition clouding. Consistent, complete thoughts were becoming increasingly difficult. Complete thoughts were reduced to atoms which disintegrated into particles which repelled one another like the same poles of two magnets, pushing them farther and farther apart. As the gap between them increased, their interplay with one another eroded until it was meaningless.

What had been clear visions within my thinking were rapidly reduced to remnants, even these becoming obscured by swirls of unrelated random thought particles scattering and separating. Gradually this maelstrom of thought particles obscured the light, leaving me in an abiding twilight without cognition, without interest, without anything—vacuity, just the void.

Chapter 7

GRANDPA'S COTTAGE AND ROMAN PURGATORY

Alice had been right: *curiouser and curiouser*.

Or maybe it had been Jerry Garcia: *…cherish well your thoughts, and keep a tight grip on your booze, 'cause thinkin' and drinkin' are all I have today.*

Only it wasn't just today. It was eternity, whatever that was. And I had no access to booze (that I knew of). And they weren't just my *thoughts*—my *thinkin'* that is: they were *me*; that's what my thoughts were; my thoughts *were* me and *I was my thoughts,* inseparably. Even without a brain to think them with, my thoughts endured. I was wrestling with my thoughts *of* my thoughts and I was losing; they nearly had me pinned. The more thoughts I had, the more thinking I did about them. And the more I thought about them, the more thinking I did. It was exquisite torture; a losing game without end. Had I gone insane? Had I gone to Hell? Were my thoughts and reality one and the same? Was I alive and condemned to thinking I was dead? Was I dead and condemned to thinking I was alive. Was I not even really thinking and just thinking that I thought? Or was I none of these and simply insane? Was I dead and experiencing this eternal torture as the penance for my sins? Surely this was Hell. It was what I deserved. I had done so much wrong.

But *what,* exactly, had I done wrong? In my physical life I had been well-raised with a firm sense of right and wrong and an empathetic relationship with others. Surely this was not a recipe for eternal damnation.

Again, I thought about my mother; surely, she would have the knowledge to ease my burden.

———————————

She was younger this time, perhaps early thirties. She was sitting on the lakeside of my grandfather's cottage at Lake Shaffer in Northern Indiana. She was wearing a one-piece swimsuit, holding a glass of Coca-Cola on ice. She and I were seated next to one another on folding lawn chairs looking out across the water. The early evening summer sun in a cloudless sky had dropped far enough that the ancient oak tree under which we sat, no longer shaded us from the sun's rays; at their lessened angle, the rays snuck below the tree's outspread branches. Grandpa's (her dad's) boat, a wooden, 17' Century Resorter, sat tied at the pier, bouncing off the bumpers, bobbing in the waves created by the weekend evening's diminishing boat traffic.

"Hi hon," she said, smiling her perpetual smile. "I wondered when you would get here. Want a Coke?"

"No…thanks," I replied. I pulled my lawn chair next to hers. It felt strange, me appearing—at least in my mind's eye—to be nearly 70 and my mom as a relatively young woman. "I…"

"You've been thinking about our last conversation; wondering how if God is the universe, what came before him."

"How did you…?"

"I'm your mother. You are a piece of me and your father. I knew the same way you would know what Chris and Greg are thinking…if you wanted to. Remember how, when you were a child, you believed I could read your thoughts? To some degree I could—all parents can. Your children thought the same of you. Parents have some ability to know their children's thoughts because their children's physical existences were derived from their own. It's just that, in our human forms, that ability is greatly reduced. In any event, as I said before, God is the sum total of everything. All that is, is a tiny fraction created from Him. And all the energy that is, is simply a small part of Him. Your thoughts are part of that energy."

"But where did that energy come from? I can accept that the universe is the sum total of the matter and the energies within it. And I can even (kind of) understand that the matter in the universe was created from that energy in some kind of big bang. But where did the energy come from? Was God created with the creation of the universe?"

Mom smiled. It was rather a knowing, loving (and slightly condescending) smile. "I recall that on my bed table, I always had a Bible; and that, whenever I visited wherever you were living after you grew up, you always had a copy of *Scientific American* or some-such magazine on yours. Which, do you think, gave a clearer answer to your question?"

"I don't know. At least *Scientific American* provided rational answers that I could at least kind of understand."

"As does faith," Mom replied. "Which is easier to understand: that God always was and always will be and that he created everything; or that the universe was created by the clustering of matter in space; and that matter was created by an explosion of energy in conjunction with something called a Boson particle; and that energy was created by conflicting forces that preceded even it; and that forces were created by something even more ancient…that they, in turn, were created by something even more ancient yet, derived from some kind of a vacuum force? The fact is: the more man learns about the mysteries of existence, the less he knows. The accumulation of knowledge creates more newer questions even as it answers fewer old ones. Only infinite knowledge can understand infinity. And infinite knowledge *IS* infinity. Infinity is God, God is infinity and only God has infinite knowledge. Everything in our experience is an infinitesimally small part of that."

"Is this real?" I asked. "I mean you and me sitting here, having this conversation."

"As real as anything you've ever experienced," Mom laughed, "and probably more so."

I reached over and took her hand in mine; it was firm yet soft...and warm; or at least it felt that way to me. I resumed our conversation. "I have another question: judging by the way you look and where we are and the wooden speedboat at the pier, I'm guessing it's around 1957?"

"July 3rd, 1957," Mom replied. "I come here often. I so love watching the fireworks at the Beach with all my loved ones. And I look forward to them tomorrow."

We sat in silence for a period, neither addressing the other; I broke it. "Sitting here, being with you, talking with you, feels like heaven to me." Mom smiled. "But I know that soon, I'll reenter the void. And that, to me at least, seems like hell. Where am I? Am I bouncing back and forth between heaven and hell? And if I am, why?"

Her smile faded, replaced by a more serious look. "I'm not qualified to tell you."

"Why not?" I questioned, my surprise and disappointment apparent in my voice. "You've always had the answers to my questions." And then the horror of my predicament dawned on me; my mother simply didn't have the heart to tell her son he had gone to hell.

"Your assumption is incorrect," she stated immediately to my unspoken revelation, again—apparently—reading my thoughts. "I am not qualified to tell you because I lack the faith necessary to do so."

"You're confusing me. What do you mean you don't have the faith? You epitomize faith. You're the most religious person I can imagine. If you can't explain it because you lack faith, can anyone?"

"Faith," she replied, "means different things to different individuals. And having faith in one truth does not necessarily mean you have faith in all truths."

Sinking deeper into my state of confusion, I was becoming increasingly desperate to understand my fate. "Then to whom do I turn to if not you? I can't spend eternity drifting back and forth between what seems like heaven and what must be hell. I've tried praying for myself and it doesn't seem like God hears me. If He does, He doesn't answer. And you tell me you can't help me because you lack the right faith. Am I lost?"

Compassion came over Mom's face as she replied: "I can assure you that I've prayed for you too and that God *did* hear me. I can only suggest that you seek the counsel of one dear to you who *has* the proper faith."

"My sister?"

"She has tremendous faith but not the type that will answer your question."

"Who then?"

"Sue," Mom replied simply.

Realizing, after my experiences that I had the capacity to meet with the pre or post-mortem Sue, I asked my mother where I should look for her. Again, her reply seemed less than satisfactory to me. "I don't have the proper faith to tell you."

"Thanks," I replied flatly.

"But I do have a recommendation: Seek her in her earthly form. From there, she can help you."

Immediately, I found myself returned to the void and just as quickly, found myself standing in Sue's darkened bedroom. I did not recognize it as anyplace I had ever been before. A simple single bed stood just feet from me. On it, beneath a pile of covers, a body stirred. As if knowing, even before sitting up or looking in my direction, she turned toward me, smiled and said, "Steve; you look no different than at our last night together. Well, maybe a little heavier," she laughed.

Sue, on the other hand, did look different than I remembered. The lines on her face were deeper and more pronounced. Her skin hung loose upon her frame and seemed to have lost its radiance. She seemed, perhaps, twenty years older than on the night of my passing. She was probably 90. I leaned down to kiss and hug her but neither of us could feel the touch of the other. I sat down upon the edge of the bed which felt quite comfortable. Curiously, the mattress beneath me did not compress from my weight.

"Where are we?" I asked.

"Joshua Arms," she replied, referring to the limited assistance elderly housing project where her dad had lived out his senior years. "After you passed, I realized I had neither the desire nor the ability to live in our house alone. I sold it and moved here."

"Are you doing OK?" I asked, concerned for her welfare.

"I'm doing fine," she replied. "Between the sale of the house and social security, I've been quite comfortable. And the residents and the staff here are great. By the way, I've still got the truck, it still runs great, and I drive at least once a week." I was impressed, both with her and with the pickup which must be nearing 40 years old by now.

I moved to hug her, again to no avail. She smiled at my effort. "Why aren't you afraid of me? I must seem like a ghost to you."

"You seem just as you always seemed to me, just a little more ethereal." She laughed. "Good choice of words, huh? I always knew I'd see you again. I just wasn't sure where or when. Living here, where so many are nearing the ends of their physical lives or have passed, one becomes a lot more familiar with the spiritual."

I pondered this for several moments before she spoke again. "There has to be a very good reason for you and me to be here together like this. What is it?"

I began to pour out for her my experiences following my passing: my dad, my mom, Buddy, the void, my last meeting with Mom, and my quest to discover my fate. I went into super elaborate detail describing my last meeting with Mom and her recommendation that I contact Sue. Her replying smile was sweet and knowing.

"Faith," she began, "at least in the sense to which you're referring, is a gift from God. It is not something you learn. It is not something you can obtain. You either have it or you don't, and, in any event, it truly *is* a gift. And just like your mom said, faith is something of many flavors. One can have faith in one aspect of religion even while questioning others. That is why your mother sent you to me to get the answer to your question as to your status. I have always had tremendous faith in most Roman Catholic traditions. She, having always been a Protestant of one denomination or another, does not. It doesn't mean that one is right and the other wrong; it's just that they differ in some respects. Lacking faith in the elements of the status of your soul, she felt I could help you and she could not."

"Fine," I said, frankly beginning to tire of her non-explanation. "So, let me ask a direct question and please keep the answer to less than book length—I don't know how long I'll be here; have I gone to hell?"

"No."

"OK then; I went to heaven. But I've got to tell you, it's not what I expected."

"No, you did not."

"Please don't patronize me. Then where have I gone?"

"Your soul, in Roman Catholic terms, is in purgatory. It's neither heaven nor hell. It's where almost all souls go before admission to heaven…or hell," she added uncomfortably.

"But I want to go to heaven. I deserve to go to heaven (I think). Is it something I should pray for?"

"From purgatory, you can pray for those on Earth. You can pray for others in purgatory. Or you can pray for the souls of those in heaven…even though there is no need. But you can't pray your*self* from purgatory; your prayers will not be heard."

"But then what hope do I have of ever leaving purgatory?"

"If those who have known and loved you pray for your soul, whether they are on earth, purgatory or heaven, they can all intercede on your behalf. And collectively, these intercessions can change your reality. It just depends upon how many of them there are and how hard they pray. And *that* depends on how you treated them during your life on earth. I want you to know that, to this day, decades after your passing, I pray for your soul every day."

Strangely, Sue's words somehow made sense to me and the comfort they provided was overwhelming. I began to explain to her how much she and her words meant to me. But like a flash-forward in a movie, she suddenly wasn't there. Then nothing was. Then, without explanation, my mother *was*. Again, I was sitting on the lawn chair next to her in 1957.

"What time is it?"

She glanced at her wrist. "7:35," she replied, "…more or less." She laughed a knowing laugh as if I would understand the humor of her answer.

I looked toward the yard next door. Ann, the eight-year old granddaughter of the woman who owned that cottage was standing there, stooped over a croquet mallet, at the back of her backswing…unmoving…as if she were frozen in time.

I glanced back toward the chair where Mom had been sitting.

She wasn't there.

Neither was the chair.

I turned to look for Ann. She wasn't there either.

Neither was I.

Chapter 8

SOULS KNOWN AND UNKNOWN

Alone again, as I had been for what was either a few seconds or a few millennia; I didn't know; I had no way to know; no standard against which to measure, no tempo or rhythms with which to maintain time.

I pondered the nature of my existence. My thoughts and my realities *were,* it occurred to me, one and the same. To experience something or someone from my human existence, I had only to remember; to picture it or them in my thoughts. Voila, I was there; *really* there. Not just an imagined situation but there interacting with those I loved and who loved me during my Earthly life. The hard part was being able to hold onto my thoughts long-enough for them to solidify. It seemed to me that, for reasons I did not understand and couldn't grasp, my thoughts and I were becoming disconnected. I was pulled in two directions at once; one direction took me deeper and deeper into the void. While the other took me deeper and deeper into my thoughts placing me in the company of those I had loved on Earth; it was like a new reality.

And the phenomena were not limited to people; I had been with Buddy. And I had experienced again locations, times and situations I had treasured, or which had heavily impacted me during my physical life. They weren't just apparitions. They were as real as what I had thought myself to have been as a human.

I pondered whether this new reality was limited to people and experiences I had loved or—at least—known. But what, I wondered, was the state of the multitudes of those I had *never* met yet felt acquainted with simply by knowing *of* them? What of those I had encountered but had neither loved nor hated? What of those I had hated whether by interaction or reputation.

I tried to visualize some of the most despicable individuals I could think of; visions of dictators, tyrants, gangsters, drug lords and serial killers formed in my mind and dissolved just as quickly. My mind, again, drifted aimlessly in an algae-covered Sargasso Sea of partial thoughts. I recalled a book I had read in junior high school. It affected me greatly; sweet sentiments faced with inhuman oppression and violence. My mind segued into consideration of man's inhumanity to man and the perpetrators of mass genocide. I wondered; what had happened to the soul of an ogre such as Adolph Hitler?

Most assuredly, he had gone to hell. Yet the persons I had met so far in my journey were blessed beings who had, in my opinion, most certainly gone to heaven. As I was sure *I* hadn't gone to hell, I could consider him and the evil he had loosed upon the world with impunity—I wouldn't have to interact with him. I thought about this with some relief, and thought, and thought...

———————————

The slate patio was surrounded by a hand-chiseled, ancient stone wall; low enough to permit an un-obscured, panoramic view of the Bavarian Alps, yet high enough to (hopefully) prevent one from toppling over the low wall to the valley floor hundreds of feet below.

Der Fuehrer sat there, alone, gazing out over the mountains. A tear ran down his cheek. "They love me," he said. "I have done so much for them." His voice hinted at acquiescence and somehow, at the same time, carried with it an unmistakable shred of doubt.

I stood to one side, gazing down at where he sat. I felt secure in the fact that since he had most surely gone to hell and I hadn't—at least not yet—he could not see or interact with me. I was merely an apparition drifting into his current world on silent wings, invisible to him, contained within in my innermost thoughts.

He raised his eyes, looking directly at me. "Who are you and how did you get in?" He spoke in his native German—a language I had never studied—yet I understood every word he said.

I spun and looked behind me at to whomever he was speaking. No one was there.

"You," he reiterated looking directly at me, "are you here to assassinate me? Who sent you? The communists? The capitalists? The English ruling class?"

It was seconds before I realized he not only could see me but was speaking to me. Was I surely in hell? How else could he and I be conferring?

"I'm not here to assassinate you. No one sent me. Frankly, I'm not sure how I got here; I'm not sure of anything anymore."

"*Frank*-ly…" he repeated, "that's funny. We went through them like bratwurst through a nervous colon." He laughed, a high-pitched maniacal laugh, seemingly amused by his sordid humor regarding the French. His laugh was pure evil. I didn't share his amusement.

He sat, I stood, looking at one another, both wondering why we were here, together, having this conversation. "Amerikaner?" he asked.

I nodded yes.

"You and your people are," he nearly shouted in a high-pitched voice, "the scourges of the Earth."

A curious comment, I thought, coming from the mouth of arguably the most abominable dictator the world had ever known. "And how is that so?" I asked sardonically.

"You have enslaved the masses," he continued, "with the false promise of opportunity. They work like dogs and slave like peasants, all for a few capitalists, with the insincere promise that—someday—they, too, might amass wealth."

"No one *slaves* for the capitalists," I replied harshly. "Everyone is free to leave or seek any employment they might be able to attain. And they are free, if they choose not to work for someone, to work for themselves. If they have the ability and will to do so," I added. "The operative word here is *free*. "

"The freedom to starve; the freedom to live like a serf; How can you call that freedom?"

"I'd rather be a starving free man than a well-fed slave," I replied indignantly.

"You are a slave to your commerce and to your material wants whether you recognize it or not. In my system of National Socialism, all is provided for the common good. Science has proven that to obtain the maximum benefit of each for all, careful planning is required for the group, with individual members of the group following through to the best of their abilities for the benefit of all—for the benefit of the Fatherland."

"Which Fatherland?"

"Deutschland."

"That," I replied a sneer forming on my lips, "is a problem. Of all the billions of people on the Earth, only a hand-full are native Germans. By whose decision are non-Germans entitled to less?"

"By Creation's," Hitler replied. "It is the right of the German people to rule. It is their heritage. It is part of their makeup. It is their divine right. And rule they will. They are Aryans. All that is required is proper planning…and execution." He pounded his fist on the wicker table to emphasize each point.

"Don't you mean executions," I asked, a sneer now forming on *my* lips. "And what of those Germans who have less God-given abilities than others? Are they, too, entitled to less?"

"True Aryans are superior in all ways and therefore entitled to more. Those of lesser abilities are accidents of genetic contamination. Scientifically selected breeding programs will keep them from the gene pool."

"And your gas chambers will ensure they don't poop in your pool?"

He ignored my sarcasm. "I am here to provide the master plan," he screamed, "and to implement it!" He again pounded his fist onto the table by which he sat.

"The advantage of our system," I continued calmly, "is freedom: The freedom to choose what we do, where we live, what we buy, what we make. Every one of us looks out for ourselves. And by letting our actions be guided by our own ambitions and self-interest, we are free to make both bad and good decisions. But since all our decisions are made for personal betterment and—over the long haul—the majority of these decisions are positive; on average, progress is the result for everyone. If I may quote someone you do not know and, I'm sure, never will: *A rising tide raises all ships*."

"Power," an unimpressed Hitler replied, "in your system, comes from wealth; the more power, the more wealth. The more wealth, the more power; it is a never-ending cycle of greed and concentration: the wealth and power concentrated in the hands of very few. Those with wealth seek only to hoard it and to add to it. Your entire economy is based on lies about opportunity for all while the concentration of wealth and power is among the capitalists whose only goal is the monopolistic accumulation of even more!"

"And your system," I queried, "is better because you have eliminated the capitalists and freedom and replaced them with your planners and *your* personal decisions?"

"Absolutely. Freedom, as you incorrectly call it, is inefficient and illusory. Whatever goods, services and benefits your system produces are inefficiently created, shared and distributed. Scientific planning eliminates that inefficiency. The result is the most benefit for the most persons. The necessities of life are fully provided leaving the people the opportunity to excel in higher human endeavors. In your system, artists starve. In *MY* system, the arts flourish as do those that produce them"

"...so long as they are ethnic Germans, of pure Aryan stock, members of your political party, they don't disagree with you and the results of their creativity meet your criteria?"

"Yes."

"And you have no regard for anyone outside of your group?"

"None: they are undeserving and un-entitled."

"And what of those *Germans* who disagree with your philosophy or don't measure up to your Aryan standards?"

"They need to be driven out or eliminated just like the Jews, the Slavs, the Gypsies and the other degenerates."

His words were driving me over the edge. Aggressively, I took a step towards him. "I only wish," I said in slow, measured words, "that I *had* come here to assassinate you." I could not help myself; I reached toward his throat.

Hitler leapt to his feet, the veins in his neck and forehead bulging as if ready to explode. From the right side of his belt, he withdrew from a leather holster the 9mm Luger he kept there. Pointing it at the center of my chest, his forefinger began tightening on the trigger. "I will send you to hell," he screamed. "Hell is where you belong!" Then, without any transition in mood, he began weeping. "It was so sad," he began, "such a loss. I felt so sorry for her. She was so sweet, so young. I only wish I could have saved her." Inexplicably, he re-holstered the Luger and sat again. His forearms crossed on the table in front of him, he buried his head in them, sobbing uncontrollably.

I was nonplussed, not knowing how to react to Hitler's sudden change in temperament. Clearly, he was insane. Was insanity his eternal punishment for his sins? Or was insanity the birthplace of his sins...or the result? I decided to try to speak with him calmly, rationally. "Who is it that you wanted to save?" I dared to ask.

"Her," he said, without definition. "You know her; the one in the book." There were two books lying atop the basket-weave table next to Hitler's seat. The one on top obscured the title of the book below it. From six feet away, however, I could read the top book's title: "Mein Kamp."

Slowly, so as not to startle Hitler, I walked in front of him toward the table to see the hidden book and perhaps learn of what he was speaking. But as I passed by him, he suddenly leapt to his feet. Startled I backed up preparing to defend myself. But he rushed past me, running toward the edge of the patio and threw himself over the low railing. He made not a sound as he fell the 150 feet or so to the rocks below. His impact, however, created a stomach-turning crunch.

Just desserts, I thought to myself as, totally disregarding what had just taken place I approached the table next to the now thankfully unoccupied chair. Like a suburbanite removing a dog's droppings from his front lawn, I gingerly picked up *Mein Kamp* between my thumb and forefinger vowing to wash my hands after, to reveal what was below it. The book below was a paperback, lying on its face. Picking it up, I turned it over to read the title: *The Diary of a Young Girl*, by Anne Frank. I laid the book down gently and walked back to the low wall curious as to where his body had come to rest.

It must have bounced or slid after the initial impact for I could see no evidence of the body or where it might have ended.

Having nowhere to go and no reason to stay, I turned back toward the house and saw, to my shock and dismay, Hitler seated where I had first encountered him. He seemed to be weeping. "They love me," I heard him say as again I watched a tear slither down his cheek like a sidewinder down a steep dune. Then, after a long pause: "I wish I could have saved her."

Clearly mad, he proceeded—slowly this time—to the low wall, pausing momentarily as he gazed across the valley at the mountains beyond. His head lowered, he looked down, hanging his head as he began crying...and again threw himself over the edge, screaming this time as he flew through the air, his body crushing onto the rocks below.

I faded from this reality and returned to the void questioning how someone, anyone could be possessed of so much hate.

Yet even as I sank into the nether world of the twilight, I wondered how it was that the humanity had spawned someone as sociopathic as Hitler. An even larger question, how was this madman able to get nearly 70,000,000 Germans—most of them, like anywhere, good people—to follow him.

What was it about human nature that compelled people to follow a person or a group whose actions were clearly contrary to the ideals that many in that same group held dear?

———————————————

My last class of the day had just ended. My mom's car, a '66 Plymouth Barracuda with the hottest engine offered that year (which in my seventeen-year-old mind had been *mine*), awaited me in the senior parking lot. Life was good. Dad's bakery which he was purchasing from my grandfather was doing so well that after paying all the costs, expenses *and* my grandfather, he was left with pretty big money. I benefitted from his success simply by being a member of "the lucky sperm club" as a friend had termed it. I had a girlfriend I loved, a large number of friends and was preparing to go to Indiana University the following year. I hoped to major in journalism there, continuing the love of writing I'd developed as one of the editors of our high school paper.

I walked down the long-ramped hallway, descending from the classroom section of the building toward the cafeteria. A left turn, just before the cafeteria, led out to the senior parking lot. I stepped out into the overcast weather, walking to the last row of cars, and stopping to admire my friend Pat's TR-3 Triumph. English sport cars were so different from the American cars which dominated the parking lot. Small, nimble with throaty exhausts; Pat's car had been rebuilt by him with an interior hand-cut and hand-sewn by his mom.

As I stood in admiration of his work, the distance-muted hubbub of excited male voices reached my ears. I turned my head and looked out toward the street. There, on the opposite side of the fence that separated the school property from the residences beside it, I saw a group of five guys I vaguely knew—the toughs of our class—encircling their "prey." I walked in their direction and as I got closer recognized the fellow they had surrounded.

Skinny, wearing the same long-sleeved black turtle-neck sweater he seemed to wear every day, his books were scattered upon the ground, the papers that had been contained within their pages blowing away ever-so-slowly in lazy loops.

He was crying; not loudly but obviously, his tears leaving trails down the light makeup he wore on his cheeks. He was being pushed roughly, from one side to the other of his circle of torment. I started jogging, then running toward the group. I was well-enough known that I thought they would listen to me if I asked them to leave this outcast alone.

"Is the sissy faggot crying?" one of the tormentors said to their victim as I reached them.

"Come on guys, stop it," I said firmly, as I stepped into the circle.

Surprisingly, the insults immediately stopped. The group of bullies suddenly turned into inanimate statues. I turned to the victim. "Are you, OK?"

"Why won't these assholes just leave me alone?" he asked, sniffling back the blood and mucus running from his nose.

"Are you OK?"

"Yeah, I'll heal. What'd I ever do to them? Why won't they just leave me alone?"

"Just because you're different from them," I said. "They're so insecure about themselves individually," I said, turning to look at them for impact (even though I knew they obviously did not see me), "that they have to bond with one another against anyone who's different. It ratifies them." The crowd around us remained silent. They stood in place, unmoving. "Just get the hell out of here," I urged the victim. "Run home as fast as you can and don't look back, no matter what they say to you."

"Thanks," he said. "He bent over, picked up his books ignoring the papers that had fallen from them, stepped between two of his frozen-in-place adversaries, and ran up the sidewalk as fast as his feet would take him. I couldn't help but observe that he did, in fact, run "like a girl."

No one said a word as I too, parted the crowd and walked back toward where my car was parked. I was beginning to see a pattern. Those to whom I had *not* been close existed only on the periphery of my being. Therefore, I couldn't really interact with them. I could observe them, but something prevented them and me from interacting.

Half-way back across the senior lot, I heard the commotion behind me reignite. I turned fearing that for some unknown reason, their former victim had returned for more torment. Reversing my direction, I headed back to the group. But as I got closer, I saw that they had found a new victim. He was on the ground and they were taking turns kicking him.

Again, I began jogging toward them. As I reached their circle, I barreled my way through their perimeter. Again, they became quiet, seemingly immobilized. I reached down to help up their newest victim. I grasped his hand firmly. He returned the firmness. At least he was OK. Leaning back, I pulled; he pulled and was now standing facing me. "Thanks bro'," he said. I stood there looking at him, immobilized by the shock of the face before me.

The face was mine. It was me; the seventeen year old me. His face and arms were scraped raw and bloody. Additional blood was running from his crooked, obviously broken nose. "I don't understand," I stammered.

"Me either," the youthful me said. "They were giving a lot of crap to...well, you know the guy I'm talking about...and I stepped in to try and get them to quit. Next thing I know, *he's* gone and I'm on the ground getting the shit kicked out of *me*."

He turned and walked back to my...his...our car. I followed briefly then turned and walked back towards the group of bullies. They were still standing there unmoving as I approached. Having now faced their hostility twice, I was more than casually upset...more pissed off than afraid; especially since their latest victim *was* me. If I had to fight them, so be it; I wouldn't win the fight—the odds were too great and I was too old in my present form—but I would take great satisfaction in hurting some of the assholes, if I could, before I went down; whatever the cost. If nothing else, just being more experienced than them might give me an advantage.

"What do you sons-of-bitches think you're doing?" It was not a question; it was a statement of my position and intended as a provocation to start a fight with the aggressors.

They didn't react. They didn't move. They just stood there.

I heard a snarly V-8 exhaust that I recognized. It was from the "Cherry Bomb" muffler that I'd had installed on my mom's car with my pay-check from the gas station. She'd never forgiven me for having the loud muffler installed on *her* car...but I thought it sounded great and the guy who sold it to me said its reduced back pressure would increase the horsepower (always a good thing if I encountered my favorite prey—V-8 Mustangs).

I turned and looked and saw the young me driving south on Arlington Avenue, headed home.

I again turned to the guys. They still stood there, unmoving. I pulled my arm back, as if to throw a punch at the face of the guy I knew to be their leader. He made no attempt to duck or raise his arm in defense. He just stood there, unmoving.

I dropped my own arm back down to my side.

I was beginning to understand.

With those I knew or loved as a human, I was as real to them as they were to me. But to those in whose thoughts I did not live or who did not live in mine, I was an apparition from a different time space dimension; a nonentity at least, a ghost at best. Hitler, however, even though I had not known him, lived within my thoughts as a result of the hate I felt for him. But these guys and I had no real relationship during my life. Accordingly, I did not exist to them.

I walked away into the gathering gloom.

———————————————

Again, the void: consciousness only with no thoughts possible. My reality—my thoughts, if you will—swirled about me, through me, within me, like droplets of fog settling upon my skin, absorbed into the materials of my clothes, inhaled into my lungs, producing no sensation, having no real effect. I looked about seeing only muted shapes, unrecognizable at first. Desperately, I tried to recognize them. As I focused on the shapes, they began coalescing into forms I could identify and identify with. I began to realize my surroundings.

I was in an abandoned church, ancient by Midwestern standards. It had, at one time, been sold after its congregation disbanded, the building eventually becoming an Italian restaurant. I recognized the building. Sue and I had eaten there often. It was in Plainfield, southwest of Chicago, where we had lived for a few years. Judging by the layers of dust and cobwebs everywhere, the building had set, unoccupied, for a long time.

Only the dim street lights outside, filtering through the translucent dust covering the windows, provided any illumination. It was nighttime and, judging by the dearth of traffic outside, must be very late night or very early morning. From no more than 100 feet away, I identified the mournful sound of a diesel tractor-trailer pulling away from the stoplight where a state highway intersected with the street upon which the church-cum-restaurant stood.

At first, they weren't recognizable as such; just subtle disturbances in the air; tiny compressions of air which were somehow discerned by me as sound. Slowly, they increased in amplitude until they were plainly recognizable: voices—human voices. They spoke in quiet, hushed, almost reverent tones. From my perch atop the dust and web-covered railing of the balcony overlooking the chapel/dining area, I watched them enter, as a group, eyeing what appeared to me to be a portable radio maybe twice the size of a cell phone. The leader of the group, holding the instrument, rotated her body from side to side, decreasing her arc until she was pointed in a direction immediately below me.

"It's in this direction," she said pointing, "and close, but I don't see anything."

"I don't think these gizmos work, but try moving it in a vertical arc," said a voice from the dark, at the back of the group. I recognized that voice: it was Todd, my son-in-law. For years he had been a member of a group investigating paranormal experiences; a ghost-hunter if you will.

Slowly, deliberately, the young lady leading them began moving the instrument up and down, first pointing at the floor at her feet, then straight up at the ceiling, then back down, then back up, always on a plane facing in my direction. With each vertical movement, her arc shortened. Finally, she stopped moving, the instrument and her arm—raised about 45° pointed right at me. "It's got to be right there," she said, "but I don't see anything."

"Me either," said another, all of them now looking directly at me.

"Oh my God!" said Todd, in a voice heard only by me; his companions stood as if paralyzed; no more movement, no more speech.

I'm not really sure how I felt. The emotion was, to me, almost embarrassment, as if a guest had opened the toilet door only to find me sitting on it. Todd's and my eyes were locked upon one another. I motioned with my hand for Todd to come up to the balcony and join me. He didn't move—just stood there, staring in disbelief. I stepped from the edge of the rail, out into the air and floated gently to the floor beside him. Todd, still staring as if in a trance, slowly regained his wits.

"Steve?" I nodded yes. "How…when…what happened?"

"You knew I had been sick," I replied matter-of-factly. "I guess it was worse than we thought."

"But when? I just left your house. You were recovering. I asked Sue and she said you were recovering."

"I guess you should have asked me," I replied, stifling a chuckle, "or gotten a second opinion. She's not infallible, you know; she just claims to be." I meant my comment as humor. Todd obviously did not receive it as such. He was in a state of shock.

"Wh…wh…when? How long ago?" Todd stammered.

"I'm not sure. Time really has no meaning to me anymore. What date do you have?"

"January 12."

Amazing, I thought to myself. I had moved *backward* in time. It was before I had evolved to my present state, before I had *died*. And yet, here I was, appearing to Todd as a ghost at the same time my human form was bed-ridden. I opened my arms. Todd and I shared a warm—albeit undetectable to me—embrace.

"I just don't understand," Todd said. "You're here, as a shadow, at the same time you're at home recuperating."

"Taken as a whole," I tried to explain, "existence has no such thing as distance and therefore, no such thing as time. What is time other than a measurement of how long it takes to cover a given distance? And what is distance other than a mechanism for evaluating the effect of velocity? And what is velocity except a formula for relating time and distance. None of these have any meaning on a greater than universal scale."

Todd looked at me questioningly as if trying to understand my meaning. I, myself, was unsure what I had just said, which amused me rather greatly.

"Go back to your group," I said. "It's wonderful seeing you."

Todd turned. Walking slowly, he moved back to the group, taking his former position at the rear of it. None of them had moved even an inch since I had descended from the railing. Todd, now standing with them, gave me a warm smile then was immobile as well.

Rising gently through the air, I reclaimed my perch atop the balcony railing. Now that I was farther away from the group, they again became animated.

"There! There!" Todd shouted pointing directly at me. "I'm sure I saw something there." All heads turned toward me. But almost in unison, they all agreed that they saw nothing, Todd as well.

"Is it still there?" the leader asked. "I'm still getting a reading."

Todd again fixed his eyes on me. "No," he said. "I don't see it. Whatever I thought I saw is gone now."

"Let's continue," the leader said. Single file, the group followed the leader up to the former altar, through the door, to the study behind it.

Todd, the last of the group, turned before passing through the door, gazed up at the balcony railing, shrugged his shoulders, smiled to himself and disappeared.

I glanced at the grandfather clock, broken and untended for years, standing in the back corner of the chapel/dining room. Its unmoving, slightly bent hands were locked in place for all time to come.

7:35...more or less.

Chapter 9

AGAIN, WE MEET

Again, the void; just my thoughts and I, which were, or course, of me surrounded—not by dark but—by an inexplicable, sullen, *lack* of brightness. Only this time, there were no connections between my thoughts and anything else. No contact with others. No familiar faces. No recalled places; just my essence in a sterile existence with no contamination from anyone or anything else. Not even my sense of self intruded upon me. My existence was like a piece of taffy being pulled on the machine at the state fair: a formless blob pulled, stretched, then folded back over into itself, moving but going nowhere, dynamic for no apparent purpose.

Was this now the hell to which I was doomed? And why was this hell my entitlement?

It occurred to me in a brief flash of lucidity that the void, itself, might be infinite. Without concept of time or distance how could it be measured? How *long* had I been in this state? How *long* was it to the end of wherever I was? *Long*? Was long a measure of time or distance? What were they? Were they the same? I attempted to regard time in terms of my human existence. Had I been in the void for seconds, centuries, millennia, or much, much longer? I could grasp no physical dimensions of where I was. Nothing could define for me how long I had been here or how long I would be. For that matter, where or what was "here."

Surely, this *was* hell; eternity spent in complete isolation. Eternity spent with complete sensory deprivation, absolute separation from any stimulus of any kind. I had become totally meaningless yet existed all the same. Conscious yet incapable of any action; certainly, incapable of any real, meaningful thought. This insanity was my condemnation, not just until the end of time—time no longer existed for me—but for eternity...whatever that was.

Lost in my thought fragments—lost within my essence—the gravity of my new existence descended over my consciousness like a gossamer black veil, clouding and darkening my view of everything, making it as meaningless as myself. Alone, unfeeling, unseeing, unknown, and unknowing, forever, and ever, until time's end and beyond; this was my penance. This was what I deserved for my transgressions; whatever they might have been.

In my increasingly insane thoughts, I screamed a silent scream; it was all I could do; but no one heard it, not even me.

I did not recognize the voice that occurred to me, as if in reply to my scream. And yet, somehow, it carried with it a hint of familiarity...and an implied threat behind the civility of the words with which it addressed me.

"I am," it said, "both pleased and surprised to find you here. Well, not so much surprised, I guess," the voice said. Unlike my previous encounters in which the images of my parents, Buddy or Todd had been present, this voice was disembodied, its words occurring within my consciousness without a visual reference.

"Where am I?"

"Welcome to hell," the voce said mockingly, "...maybe." The voice's chuckle, although unheard, somehow entered my perceptions.

My very existence was rocked. It was what I suspected but had denied to myself. Surely it wasn't true. "Where the hell am I?"

"Exactly," was the voice's too-short response. Subdued, taunting laughter followed the terse reply and sunk into me like the chill from an icy wind.

"Who are you?"

"You know me. You hate me." The familiarity of the voice grew within me. "As I said, welcome to hell; my own private hell. Although you're now included in it, you lucky son-of-a-bitch, so I guess it's not so private anymore." The words were followed by another laugh; a hideous, leering, frightening laugh that singed my soul.

I probed my deepest memories. I *knew* the voice. I recognized the attitude; down-home yet suave and intelligent, with a subtle hint of threat hidden behind what was clearly a bright pastel façade of friendliness, covering the darkest of shades.

"Why can't I see you?"

"Trust me; I'm sure you don't want to. I'm hidden in your memory...a repressed memory, if you will." Again, the hideous laugh.

"Who are you?" I demanded.

"A member of your family. We got along."

"Then why can't I see you?"

"Because you really don't want to...and, frankly, I don't want you to either."

"Don't tease me. Show yourself."

"Trust me; you don't want to see me. You would see me only as you remember me in your thoughts. The thoughts are not pleasant and neither would be your vision of me. If you were to see me, you would find yourself quite repulsed. That is because you hate me. Do you know *why* you hate me?"

I would not dignify that rhetorical question with a reply. The disembodied voice, however, continued as if I had answered. "For humans, there are only four resolutions to conflict: murder, suicide, apology or forgiveness. Think about that. It's quite true. I chose the first two." Again, the maniacal laugh burst into my mind.

A spark of recognition flickered in my thoughts but quickly extinguished even as I tried to fan it to life. I looked behind me, in front of me, toward both sides but saw nothing. "Is it really so important for you to see the image of one you hate?" the voice asked. "Your hate is the reason you are here. Your hate is the reason *I* am here."

Like the slowly gathering light of pre-dawn, the realization slowly, imperceptibly grew within me; the familiarity of the voice; conflict; murder and suicide; a family member? I knew and now I could look. I spun and there he was, immediately behind me, so close that our eyes—at least what was left of his—were nearly pressed together.

Raw flesh, sinew and bone fragments hung like Spanish moss from the bones of his face. A single tooth, still attached to decayed remnants of fleshy gum tissue, swung like a pendulum from the lower left of his grotesquely deformed jawbone. Chin, lips, nose and left eye were intact. His right eye, the forehead above it and perhaps a fourth of his cranium, back to his right ear were missing. A grey mass of brain tissue spilled over the edge of the missing skull bone, hanging down, mingling with blood hair and other bone fragments, covering his right ear and cheekbone. Billy's face, what was left of it, showed no emotion.

I screamed in horror. If I were still capable, the sight would have made me physically ill. As it was, only my consciousness regurgitated.

In the eye of my consciousness, I recalled the scene as my sister had described it to me. It was permanently burned into my psyche like a glowing branding iron into a yearling steer's hide. My thoughts drifted back to unsuccessfully repressed memories of what my sister had told me:

> It was early morning. Jerry had just left their lakeside condo for the long commute to work in Indianapolis. Dawn (her daughter, recently estranged from Billy) and Dawn's infant son were upstairs in their bedroom.
>
> Assuming the ring of the doorbell to be a neighbor, my sister opened it to find Billy standing there. Ominously, he said nothing. He simply stared at her in stone-faced, foreboding silence. My sister spoke first: "Dawn is still in bed."
>
> "Go get her."
>
> "She was up most of the night with the baby. I'll tell her you came…" Glancing down, she saw the gun in Billy's hand. Immediately, Cheryl attempted to shut the door.
>
> With no further words, Billy pushed through the door, pushed the barrel of the pistol into Cheryl's torso and pulled the trigger. The bullet tore through her abdominal muscles, missed her spine by the narrowest of measures and exited her back taking a small piece of her liver and a large volume of skin, organ, and muscle tissue with it, leaving bacteria-laden shreds of her blouse lining the tunnel left by the bullet's passing. She was knocked to the floor by the impact and lay there in shock. Shaking, Billy stood over her delivering a barrage of profanity at her, aimed the gun at her head and fired a second time.
>
> Dawn came running down the staircase and saw her apparently dead mother on the floor. She ran towards her.
>
> Billy's shot dropped Dawn beside her prone mother. He shoved the revolver's muzzle hard against her temple and fired again.

Having apparently killed both of them, he ran up the stairs to the bedroom, grabbed the baby, charged back down the stairs, then slowed down lest he call attention to himself, walked calmly to his waiting car, placed the baby carefully on the seat, belted him in as best he could, and drove away.

But the second bullet Billy had aimed at my sister's head at nearly point-blank range, had miraculously missed its mark, the bullet nicking her ear as it passed through her hair and into the floor. The concussion immobilized her even further. Lying on the floor, facing the body of her murdered daughter, fearing for the life of the baby, she knew she must act. She tried to rise but was unable to even set up.

With neighbors leaving for work there was activity outside. With superhuman effort using her knees and elbows as the only means of propulsion, she agonizingly dragged her way to the still open front door (Billy in his haste had not latched it), crawled onto the porch and was able to attract the attention of neighbors who called EMS and the police.

The rest of this incident, as surely burned into my memory as the portion told me by my sister, was learned by me from my father and newspaper reports of the police action.

The police, questioning my sister even as the EMS people frantically tried to save her life, got a description of Billy's car and—learning from my sister that he might be headed to his parents' house in Carmel, IN—dispatched a helicopter along the most likely route. The State Police helicopter quickly identified what was likely the perpetrator vehicle and coordinated patrol cars on the ground. As had been suspected, Billy drove to his parent's house and parked the car in the driveway.

Billy moved the baby to the back seat and was shortly joined in the front seat by his father. His father was concerned over what might have happened to precede Billy's arrival at his house with the baby but without the mother. They were engaged in some sort of deep conversation as several policemen and a female officer, all out of Billy's sight, took up concealed positions around the car, their guns drawn and ready. In order to get Billy's attention, an officer, with gun holstered and hands raised, revealed himself to Billy in front of the car and attempted to speak with him. As Billy focused on the officer in front, the female officer crept up to the car's back door, jerked it open, snatched the baby and ran for cover.

Billy's hand immediately went to the waistband of his pants. Grabbing the Colt, he placed the barrel under his jaw, the muzzle pointed up toward his brain, and pulled the trigger for the last time.

"Why?" I asked. "Why did you do it?"

"We were in conflict," he answered matter-of-factly. "Neither Dawn nor I were capable of apologizing or forgiving at the time. What I did was the only resolution left to me."

"You arrogant asshole. She had done nothing wrong except to forgive you, time after time. For that, you murdered the woman who had borne your son and tried to kill her mother—my sister—who had never done anything except to try to right what was wrong between you and her daughter."

"I always assumed that would be your position," Billy said coolly. "At least, now, we have plenty of time to attempt to resolve the conflict between us;" again, the maniacal laugh. "And, as we're already dead, murder or suicide are out of the question, so it looks like all we can do is apologize and forgive." Again, the laugh.

I reached out as if to clench my fingers around his throat and rip the remains of his head from his body but it was like air grasping air. He vanished from my view. His voice, however, remained like the disembodied smile of the Cheshire cat. "Plenty of time," he added again before beginning that same laugh anew. Strangely, rather than maniacal, the laugh was merely whimsical this time.

"Plenty of time," he repeated. My fingers were empty. He was gone. Yet his voice continued, more faintly now. "You know why you and I are here?"

I chose not to answer.

"Hate," the disembodied voice answered for me. "I am here because of the hate others felt for me."

"Felt?"

"Others have forgiven me. You *still* hate me."

"You would expect less?"

"No, I considered the hate to be well justified. I even hated myself. But in time, the others were able to forgive me which allowed me to find peace with myself...to some degree," he added before laughing again. "When one is hated by others, it is impossible to find personal peace. Without personal peace, it is impossible to find peace with God. Without peace with God, there is nothing. Hate prevents both the hater and the hated from finding peace."

"You're saying I am here because I hate you?"

"I'm saying hate and peace cannot coexist and without peace, one cannot find one's place with God."

"Go to hell."

"Been there, done that, bought the T-shirt;" again the detestable laugh. "See what I mean?"

Chapter 10

LIFE, "DEATH BY RELIGION," AND SALVATION

Is free will a physical attribute or a condition of being? Without a physical presence with which to manifest one's will, does it even exist? All I can say is that, with all my will, I wanted to be away from the essence of the being who had murdered my niece. Anything, *anything,* I thought, was preferable to being in his company. I prayed for my existence to be separated from his.

And it was. Again, like a veil, the void fell over me and surrounded me.

The void this time, whatever time is, was subtly different however. It was still the void—no sound, no movement, no visual distraction, no feeling, no involvement—and yet there was something different about it. For seconds (or centuries) I pondered the situation, trying to define the difference. It certainly wasn't the light; there was none. But perhaps therein was the key. The *darkness* seemed to have lessened.

I tried to relate my current situation to my earthly experience. It was like being outside, in a dark countryside, under an overcast of clouds, on a moonless, pitch-black, summer night. With the approach of dawn still many minutes away, the sunlight below the horizon was beginning to illuminate the overcast in the sky from *below* the horizon, its dim light reflected to earth from the bottoms of the clouds overhead. What emerged below them wasn't light as we knew it, but rather a lessening of the darkness. We still couldn't see much and yet could perceive of our growing ability to do so soon. Somehow, though still in the dark, the promises of enlightenment and hope were revealed by the diminished dark.

My thoughts were random and partial. I knew I was in the void which terrified me. I desperately wanted out. I also knew that I was closer to its inner boundaries—the boundaries which separated me from the center; from heaven; from the Creator. I could sense this from the lessened darkness. And that provided me at least a modicum of hope.

Brief recollections appeared to me like fireflies on a warm July evening: illuminating, becoming visible to me, then extinguishing, leaving me alone in the dark again. I fought to grasp one of my passing thoughts while it still shone. If I could grasp it, it would at least give me a brief reprieve from the void. But my efforts were in vain; As soon as my thoughts illuminated, they immediately extinguished and were gone.

One after another, memories, theories, people, situations, things previously treasured and things previously ignored, blinked into and out of my awareness. With the departure of each, I reentered the void, for an interminable period. I desperately tried to pray for a whole and continuing memory to lift me from my isolation; but prayer required a completeness of thought of which I was incapable. I tried searching whatever recollections I could muster for something tangible that I could grasp and hold onto; anything that had impacted me, ever.

———————————————

"Did you see that?" The question was whispered.

It was unseasonably cool. The storm clouds had broken and scattered with the sunrise. The risen sun showed pink through the increasingly scattered low fluffy clouds. Thoroughly soaked, I crouched at the base of a majestic oak tree. For safety and to keep the just-passed precipitation from flowing down the bore, I kept the muzzle of my single-shot .22 Savage rifle pointed at the ground. "There," the voice whispered again, an outstretched, arthritis-bent index finger pointing up an adjacent oak tree.

I raised my ten year-old eyes along the sightline indicated by my grandfather. As I did so, I saw the long-dried and brown—but now water-covered and glistening—oak leaf spiraling rapidly downward. Mom's dad continued his whispered tutelage. "Where do you think a dried dead leaf comes from in early fall when there's no wind?" I raised my gaze further and saw it; near the treetop, but far enough down to be protected from hawks by surrounding limbs and foliage: a large squirrel nest built from twigs and dried leaves. "They're in there to get out of the rain," Grandpa continued. I strained to hear his near-silent words. "Just shows they've got more sense than we do. They're warm and dry sitting inside their nest and we're out here, freezing our butts off, soaked to the bone. Now that the rain's stopped, they're moving around, getting ready to come out to look for food. That's how they knocked that leaf down. You best get ready."

Sliding the bolt forward and rotating it to finish cocking the rifle, I took a position, leaning up against a tree trunk for support to stabilize my aim. Just as Grandpa had shown me, I took aim, centering the tiny dot at the end of the barrel into the bottom of the "V" of the dovetail sight atop the breach, near my face, lining both up with where my target would shortly be. At that distance, I had been trained, the edge of the dot should be as low as possible in the V, but with all of it being visible there. My line of sight and the rifle were aimed just above the horizontal branch supporting the nest. A squirrel would soon make the fatal mistake of appearing on the limb on the side of the nest closest to the trunk. I would go for a body shot; to the lungs and heart.

Cautiously, taking a few quick steps, stopping, standing, looking, then back onto all fours taking a few more steps, a large grey squirrel began his journey across the limb. "As soon as he stops, squeeze the trigger; don't jerk it. But do it quickly so you get him before he starts moving again."

The squirrel stopped then stood on his hind legs to look around. I gently pulled the trigger. But aside from a near-silent click, nothing happened. I glanced over at my Grandpa. His eyes rolled back in his head and he whispered a curse. "Fuck a duck," he whispered. "You didn't load it." I stifled a laugh. I had never heard my grandfather drop the "F" bomb before. That he now felt able to do so in front of me must mean that he now considered me an adult. Somehow, even though I knew the use of such a word was wrong, that made me proud.

Feeling like an idiot—albeit a more adult one—I slid the bolt open, inserted a .22 long rifle hollow-point, slid the bolt forward, locked it and resumed my position. Surprisingly, the squirrel was still there, still standing on his hind legs. Without further instruction, I aimed carefully and squeezed the trigger. With a sharp rap and minimal kick, the little Savage rifle spit out its small projectile, knocking the squirrel off the limb. I opened the bolt on the now-empty rifle as a safety precaution, leaned it up against the tree and ran to where the squirrel had fallen, some 25 yards away. The bullet had passed through his chest and out his back obliterating his heart in the instantaneous process. The entry wound was barely visible. The exit wound was a gaping mass of torn flesh. The squirrel was no more.

I ran back to my granddad. "I killed it with one shot," I said proudly.

"Where is it?" He was still whispering.

"Still under the tree."

Without a further word, Grandpa rapped me hard on the back of my head with his knuckles.

"Ouch! Why'd you do that?" I said under my breath.

"You just killed one of God's creatures." He was no longer whispering. "Killing for the joy of killing is sick, do you understand? You don't ever shoot a living creature except to eat it or keep it from killing you. Now go get it and stick it in your game bag." Did the fact that he was no longer whispering mean the hunt was over? The answer came soon enough.

On the long walk back through the woods, across a couple of cornfields, and up the road to where my grandfather's '59 Mercury station wagon was parked, no words were exchanged. It seemed the longest, most uncomfortable walk of my life. I lowered my head feeling what I now recognized as well-deserved shame.

"By the way," Grandpa added, breaking the ominous silence a few feet from the car, "nice shot."

My spirits were rejuvenated. My chest swelled with pride; a compliment from a man who was surely the smartest in the world—at least in my immediate world.

———————————————

Grandpa instructed me how to clean and prepare the squirrel for cooking. I didn't enjoy it. Aside from the mess from gutting and skinning the carcass, I couldn't help but look into the eyes of the decapitated head as it laid beside the cutting board, looking at me, a single unspoken question appearing to me in its now-dull, wide eyes: why?

Once the carcass was fully cleaned and rinsed, Grandma put the parts into a buttermilk-filled bowl then placed the bowl into the refrigerator. After an hour or so, she removed them, patted them dry with a towel, coated them with seasoned flour and pan-fried them. When we sat down to dinner that evening, Grandma and Grandpa had hamburgers (my favorite) and I had the squirrel. I didn't care much for it and only took a bite or two.

But it didn't go to waste. The rest of my dinner was taken out to the kennel to the beagles which ate it with abandon, bones and all.

After dinner, I sat down to watch "Walt Disney's Wonderful World of Color" on TV. Featured that night was a cartoon starring Chip 'n Dale—chipmunks although, tails notwithstanding and artistic license being what it is, they *could* have been squirrels. It seemed as I looked at them that they were repeating the question of their dead cousin: why?

I never went squirrel hunting again because I knew I didn't want to eat one. But I gained a newfound appreciation that day—at just ten years of age— of life and death.

———————————————————

Somehow, my thinking continued, along lines only loosely related. From life and death, it segued into recollections of the 9/11 attacks; from there into considerations of Islam; from there into my studies of history centering on the Crusades of the middle ages; and from there to a college lecture I had once endured. Focusing on my fleeting recollections of the lecture from many years back, saved me from reentering the void to which I otherwise would have been condemned.

Always a T.A., never a professor when you're a freshman, I thought to myself as we awaited his appearance at the podium in the large lecture hall. Barely older than those they taught, I felt Teaching Assistants' thinking to be immature; rather than a launch platform for their or their students' further thoughts, they delivered lectures which were simply the regurgitation in rote of what they had previously read or been taught. This one was to be no different: "Throughout the course of history," he began—no doubt the same line with which he opened each and every boring lecture he gave—"there have been many causes of war and conflicts. But can you guess what—by a very wide margin— has been the most prevalent of these?"

The hand of a girl—skinny, straight waist-length hair, a hippy-looking chick (socially, not anatomically)—went up in the air. She wore a baggy, loose, purple angora turtle-neck sweater hanging over tight blue jeans tucked into knee-length fringed boots. Granny glasses and a red beret completed her outfit.

"The young lady in the fourth row," the T.A. said, pointing directly at her.

"Religion!" she exclaimed, with the passion of an eyewitness identifying a murderer. "The Romans invading England to spread Christianity to the pagans, the Europeans invading the Middle East where Christians, Jews and Moslems all claimed holy lands, the Spaniards invading Central and South America to convert the natives to Catholicism, Protestants and Roman Catholics forever warring in Ireland, the U.S. propping up a Roman Catholic dictator in Buddhist South Viet Nam, the..."

"*Quite right,*" *the T.A. cut her off.* "*There is no need to continue…we'd be here for the rest of the semester.*" *A chuckle arose from the young audience.* "*Ironic, isn't it? Organized religion has been the primary cause of wars throughout the history of mankind.*" *A skinny kid to my right waved his hand frantically.* "*Yes sir,*" *the T.A. said, acknowledging him.*

"*I grant you,*" *the young man said,* "*that religion may have been a factor in many wars, but it is a long leap from being a factor in many to being the primary cause of all. I question the basis of your assumption.*"

"*Your name sir?*"

"*Jim Sebastian.*"

"*May I ask you your year and major if you've declared, Mr. Sebastian?*"

"*Sophomore. Economics.*"

"*Well Mr. Sebastian, as an aspiring economist, I've sure you view world history from an economic standpoint. After all, when you are a hammer, the world is a nail. [An approving murmur from the crowd] However, as a student of sociology, I approach the causal factors of war from a more humanistic standpoint. After all, war is the most abhorrent form of human behavior. And in my nearly seven years of study in my field, I can assure you that religion is the greatest cause, without a doubt. Let us move on.*"

"*But…*"

"*Let us move on.*"

"*But…by whose definition is war man's most abhorrent behavior? Genocide has been performed outside of war. Forced starvations, for instance, have…*"

"*We will now move on!*"

Sebastian's hand was again waving wildly. The T.A. again acknowledged him with a comment: "*I have a lot of material to cover today regarding the social basis of war. I will permit you your question, but first wish to precede it with a question for you: I defy you; can you name anything good that ever came out of any war? No, I didn't think…*"

Before the T.A. had finished his response to the answer Sebastian had not been permitted to give, Sebastian spoke loudly, cutting the T.A. off, so everyone in the hall could hear: "*Peace,*" *he answered,*" *is a welcome result of any proper war. That's one good thing that comes out of war. Or an end to slavery, or the development of new medical procedures or…*"

Laughter rippled through the audience. The T.A.'s scathing glance cut both the laughter and Sebastian's answer off.

I noted that the T.A. provided no factual argument to any of Sebastian's disagreements. I also noted that when Sebastian gave the T.A. his name, the T.A. had promptly wrote something—no doubt the name—down.

The guy seated to my immediate left poked me in the ribs with his elbow. I turned to see a smirk on his face. "There went an 'A'," he said, under his breath, referring to damage that Sebastian had just done to his course grade. He followed with a soft chuckle.

I nodded my head in agreement. How, I wondered, could this be happening at an institution where people were supposed to be taught critical thinking? We were supposed to learn how *to think; not* what *to think. Unfortunately, it was the same way at almost all centers of higher learning.*

My thoughts drifted from this long-ago scene and back to the emptiness…but not for long.

The void wasn't as empty, not as desolate, and not as permanent as before. Somehow, I retained recollections of my previous thoughts. And these continued growing into considerations of life and death, war, and peace, good and evil, God and Satan; their meanings and places.

It was a Saturday, noontime, at the old Indiana University Extension building on the near north side of downtown Indianapolis. I sat with two of my classmates at the first-floor café where we all gathered for cokes, coffee or, if we had sufficient funds, lunch.

I had just sold my Honda Super Hawk motorcycle, which I'd ridden since 1966 to one of the guys at the table. He kept bragging about how much faster it was than his buddy's Super Hawk. I hadn't told him, during the negotiations for the sale of the bike, about the radical modifications I'd made to the engine, for fear he wouldn't buy the bike if he knew I'd done major work on it myself. Now, at least, I felt safe in letting him know. "I put a 350 kit in it. Had everything balanced. Then a Webcor cam. Gutted the mufflers for less back-pressure. Then I re-jetted it to get the right air/fuel ratios into it."

"That explains a lot," he said. "If it was still yours and you wanted to make it more competitive on the drag strip, what would you do next?"

"Head work," I replied immediately, having considered his question months before selling the bike. "I know a guy who does a great job of milling heads and "flowing" them so they can really breathe. All you've got to do is pull the heads and take them to him…oh, yeah; and pay him or he won't give them back."

"Would you be interested in doing some more work on my bike?"

"Man, I'd love to but between work and school and the baby, I don't have much time."

"I'll pay you," he offered.

My ears perked up.

The wall-mounted television above us was blaring out the voice of Secretary of Defense McNamara as he described the progress our troops were making at Quong Tri. "Lies! Lies! Lies! Turn that liar off!" screamed a kid in the corner, wearing a tattered camouflage shirt. It was common knowledge that he'd lost a leg in Viet Nam. Without hesitation my motorcycle's new owner stood atop our table, reached up and switched the TV off.

The guy in the corner didn't say thank you. But he did stop screaming—thankfully.

Everyone in the cramped room ignored the incident. Nam vets were common in the hallways of the campus. Some of them were normal enough, some of them were nuts; the important thing was not to provoke them enough to find out who the nuts were. Some were like short-fused sticks of dynamite.

Father Flipout, as most referred to him, entered the room struggling courteously through the crowd, smiling and apologizing, obviously looking for a pathway to our table.

"This is all your fault, asshole," the guy sitting to my immediate right said, ducking his head so the good Father couldn't read his lips. "All you had to do was ignore him the first time he showed up. But no-o-o-o-o-o-o; you had to engage him in conversation and now we have to put up with his shit every time we come in here." His smirk melted into a smile, just so I would know he was kidding me. I returned his smile.

"I'm not kidding he screamed." My smile faded immediately. Then he smiled again. "Just kidding," he said. I smiled as I gave him a good-natured punch in the shoulder. Being raised Protestant I respected Father Flipout for being a man of the cloth even if I didn't buy into Catholicism. And I enjoyed our conversations.

The priest—at least we all assumed he was a priest because he wore a Roman collar and black hassock—squeezed into the remaining chair, trapped between our round table and the corner of the café. Slightly built to the point of being skinny, his neatly trimmed beard had hints of grey at either side of his chin, incongruous with the relative youth of his unlined face.

"Good morning gentlemen," he said as he sat. He spoke with just a hint of Irish brogue.

"*And top-o-the mornin' t' ya'*," *said Alvin seated opposite him, badly faking an Irish accent as best he could, handicapped by his Southern Indiana twang.* "*And the topic of today's sermon is…?*"

The presumptive priest looked around our table, smiling at each of us in turn before speaking. It was impossible not to return the warm smile no matter how we felt about sharing his company. "*No sermon men,*" *he replied.* "*I'm just grateful being able to share your company on this beautiful day.*" *His attitude exuded a love for life which was difficult to challenge.*

The veteran on the opposite side of the room stood and with the aid of a single crutch made his way toward the exit. The priest, seated in the corner, could not help but see him. He offered a smile and a friendly wave. The veteran, looking directly at him, did not acknowledge the smile or the wave. The priest waved a second time. The veteran gave him the finger and left without speaking. From my position, I saw both parties' non-verbal exchanges with the other. I felt sorry for the priest and restrained anger towards the veteran.

"*He had no right to do that,*" *I offered, attempting to assuage whatever pain the veteran had inflicted.*

"*It may not have been a response that I would have recommended,*" *Father replied still smiling,* "*but he certainly did have a right to express himself. He is burdened. How would you feel in his position?*"

"*Hoo-boy; here we go again…*" *Alvin said as he stood up and headed toward the door.*

"*And so my son,*" *the priest began, ignoring Alvin's departure,* "*how goes your life today?*"

"*Same-o, same-o. Go to work, go to school, go back to work, go home, take care of the baby while the wife goes to school, sleep, go to work. At least I get Saturdays off. Pretty exciting life, huh?*"

"*Certainly a very blessed one,*" *he replied.* "*A wife, a child, a job, a home, an education; all this at such a young age…you're very lucky.*"

"*I'll feel a lot luckier when I get my degree and can start working more at a paying job. I just had to sell my motorcycle to keep up with our debts.*"

"*Congratulations on being able to keep up with them; for that, you can be grateful.*"

Rightfully, I felt, I could have been pissed off at the priest's cavalier attitude regarding my life's drudgery, my personal finances, and the motorcycle I so dearly missed. But I wasn't. In fact, I appreciated his perspective. Everyone had problems in their lives and mine were a lot less than some.

————————————

I learned that the good Father (I refused to refer to him as Father Flipout) was the administrator and a resident of a half-way house for recovering alcoholics and drug addicts just a couple of blocks from the extension campus. His regular visits to our school were both professional—drug use among the students was not unheard of and alcohol consumption was a norm—and evangelistic, reaching out as a missionary to the students.

Although fashionably agnostic at that age I spoke with him often on a variety of subjects, religious philosophy being one of them. It was during the summer session that year—my last before earning my degree—that he sat down beside me as I took lunch. The television—as it had been for the last few days—was filled with the horror of the slaughtered Israeli Olympic athletes in Munich by Muslim terrorists. Without so much as a greeting to him, I began: "Those bastards," I said, referring to the terrorists who had been the perpetrators. "The only way this is going to end is for us to bite the bullet, so to speak, and then put it through their heads. It's interesting," I continued, parroting the lecture I'd suffered and disagreed with just a few years before, "that most wars have resulted from religion. So many Moslems just seem to glorify in it."

Per usual, the good Father smiled before commenting: "All that formal religions do is to try to connect us with the creator in ways we can understand. All of them are looking for humanity's place in a larger mystical realm. That realm is mystical because it is beyond the comprehension of human beings. That is the reason Jesus Christ was sent to us as a human being; to put that mysticism into terms to which we could relate."

I could tell already, this was going to be one of those interesting philosophical conversations/debates that both of us seemed to enjoy. "So you're saying that all religions have credibility? That Buda is as relevant as Jesus Christ? That all of them are equally to blame for wars?" He knew and I knew that I was baiting him with my questions.

Again, he smiled. "All people and religions are a part of God, some just more so than others. Some, being more divinely inspired, are a much larger part of Him than others. Were prophets such as Isaiah, Ezekiel or John the Baptist divinely inspired? Absolutely. Was Mohammed? Was Buda? The answer, again, is yes. Do all religions have the same credibility? Is Buda as relevant as Jesus Christ; No, at least certainly not to Christians."

I found his first comments to be acceptable to my personal philosophy. I found his ending comment to be confusing. Before I could question it, he continued:

"Jesus Christ was truly the Son of God. As such, he is a much larger portion of God than all the prophets, all the holy men, all the people on the face of the earth ever, no matter how divinely inspired they might be.

Are religions to blame for wars? All of them seek a path toward enlightenment—the understanding of God. And that path, universally, is peace and love. All religions promote the benefits of peace and love for one another. And they all seek to answer three universal mysteries: from where do we come, what are we doing here, and where are we going. But religions are the interpretations of the Holy Mysteries by man. As such, all of them are subject to misinterpretation...and to manipulation," he added with a wink. "All religions can—and have—been perverted for the convenience of mankind's purposes— whatever those purposes might have been at the times of those perversions. The philosophies predominating at any given time, in any given culture, dictate how religion is interpreted."

I sat there for a few moments which seemed an eternity, before replying. "What about non-Christians?" I asked. "Can they, too, go to heaven?" I couldn't help but break into a grin as I voiced a cliché because it was true: "Some of my best friends are Jewish."

His ever-present smile seemed to broaden. "As are mine. All people are imbued with a degree of divinity by their Creator—and always have been. That is what makes them people and not just hairless apes. Well relatively hairless," he added directing my attention with his eyes to the bearded hippie with shoulder blade-length hair and equally long beard standing by the door. We both chuckled. "Jesus was sent here to help us find the way to salvation. And that way is through peace and love for one another."

"Being as you're a professed Christian and a Roman Catholic priest, you've said exactly what I would expect. I'll give you credit: you know what side your bread is buttered on. So you're saying that non-Christians can have life everlasting?"

"All of human spirit is eternal, irrespective of one's accepted religion. The question is, will eternity be spent in damnation or with the Creator. In Judaism, there is a concept called Scheol. In its simplest interpretation, it's the land of the dead. In others, however, it's synonymous with the concept of Hell. In the latter interpretation, it's to be forgotten—or forced from the minds—of those left behind after death."

"So, you're suggesting that Jesus Christ and Christianity are simply the byproducts of the culture at the time of his life on Earth?" Again, I tried to throw him a curve ball.

He smiled: a very knowing, very sincere smile. "Jesus Christ was the only human sufficiently divine to be the Son of God. He is a part of God just as you are a part of your parents. He was sent to Earth to show us—as humans—the pathway to heaven and to provide us with salvation from our sins. His message and his actions were spread throughout the entire known world and recorded in divinely inspired written word for posterity. But his larger message was quite simple: do good. Do you believe this?"

"Of course; I was raised Christian."

"That's not what I asked. Do you BELIEVE this."

I hesitated. "Yeah, I guess."

He paused, a knowing smile on his face. "Then let me ask you another question. Do you LIVE your life according to the Christian ideals to which you were raised? Do you love your neighbor as yourself? Do you share your love—through your actions—with all you meet? Do you forgive those who, in any way, may have hurt you? Can you find love in your heart for those who have wronged you?"

"That's quite a mouthful, Father. Any chance you could just hit me with one question at a time and then wait for an answer?"

"Yes, it was. I'm sorry. I'm not trying to corner you with my questions. My concern for you—above and beyond the fact that I enjoy our conversations—is the same as it is for everyone. I'm concerned that your soul will find its eternal place with God. Do you have any questions for me?"

I didn't have another question. I was too busy contemplating what the priest had just said to think of one.

Chapter 11

MORALS ABORTED

I didn't realize I had returned to the void until my thinking resumed, removing me from it. My consciousness had been there for time-immeasurable; my essence had languished there, aware only of its existence and nothing else. The hell of being without—without substance, without meaningful consciousness, without stimulation, without contact with others—condemned me to some vacuous cavity suspended in an empty reality. And yet, respite could be accomplished when a thought flickered, providing me with me again with a modicum of consciousness--if only I could hold onto it long enough to ignite its flame.

————————————

Politics and politicians: in my life on Earth I had abhorred them even as they had fascinated me. I had observed them with rapt attention—and disgust. To my way of thinking, politics was nothing more than a mechanism for one human trying to exercise power and control over another without having to confront them head-on, safe behind a systematized barrier which was itself, politics created by politicians for the own perpetuation.

My consciousness was jolted out of the void by this sudden consideration of politics. I tried to recall aspects of them that had held my attention during Earth-life. My rambling recollections, however, were as ethereal as individual molecules of water vapor. I pondered this: The molecules were water, of course—all the necessary elements were there, bonded into a single entity—but they were not recognizable or usable as such. I fought to concentrate, to dwell long enough on this to lift me more fully from the void. My spirit's ramblings segued from politics, to water vapor, to humidity, to sunny summer days; Humid, hot, moisture(water)-laden air near the ground, created discomfort; Being less dense than the cooler air above it, the warm surface air would rise, a vertical wind creating low pressure at ground level. As the air rose, it cooled until it could no longer contain the moisture it had contained so effortlessly when warmer. As altitude increased and temperature decreased, the vapor would coalesce into drops of real water, as we knew it on Earth. As these drops clung to one another and gained mass, they were no longer able to be suspended in the air around them. They precipitated from the heavens to sustain physical life on the surface of the land below even as they cooled the air close to it. It was a never-ending cycle...as was all of existence—in whatever form.

Likewise, my thoughts from the void were vaporous, without recognizable form, pattern, or substance. Occasionally though, for reasons I did not grasp, something would cause them to condense, coalescing into conscious bits of rationality, removing me—albeit temporarily—from the void and giving meaning to my spiritual existence. The longer I could hold on to them, the more substance my thoughts contained until they obtained recognizable, familiar patterns which became memories. My recognition of these thoughts provided a foundation which would allow them to build upon themselves providing a continuing direction and salvation from the void.

Conscious thoughts provided my soul with release. Just as they were now doing with politics. I wondered to myself, how was it that my irrational spirit could move from thoughts of politics, to the physics of rain, to the spirituality of existence? Was it that insertions into politics by topics such as abortion, or individuals' sexual orientations, or anything regarding politics (or, for that matter, any thoughts we had) were built upon rational processing of memories which preceded them? Were not rational thoughts the basis of our God-connected existence? Why not spiritual considerations? Why not something outside the realm of our earth-bound physical life?

Again, my thoughts comingled, each building upon the skeleton of the one before it, creating a foundation for further thinking. I found myself, again, with my mother; me in my early 20s, she around 50 years of age. A couple, both dear friends had informed me of the unplanned pregnancy they were sharing. I had been asked to stand up with them at their hastily planned wedding. "What do you think they should do?" I asked. "Marry and start a family? Have the baby and give it up for adoption? Abort?"

"You disappoint me," Mom replied matter-of-factly.

The curtness of her reply surprised me. I looked up at her face. Her eyes, her facial expression, offered a look that stood somewhere between resignation and disappointment for my friends, anger with me and disgust with everything I had just said. I tried to choose my next words carefully so as not to cause any further upset. It would have been better had I said nothing. "Things have changed," I offered, "from when you were young. It's no longer necessary for people to have unplanned babies. Birth control pills should have prevented this. But they didn't. Why should either of them have their hopes and dreams for the future put on hold or destroyed by an unplanned, unwanted child? And why should she have to risk her life bearing a child for which they are ill-prepared to provide at this point?"

I couldn't help but notice Mom's pupils dilate as the anger briefly flashed again in her eyes. But her fierce expression quickly softened. She began with a question: "How do you explain the miracle of human birth? Why, for that matter, do we even regard it as a miracle?"

Still picking my words with care so as not to inflame her, I tried to answer as candidly as possible. "I'm not really sure," I stammered, "that in this day and age, it's really considered to be a miracle."

Her eyebrow arched: "Oh—what changed?"

"The biology, the chemistry, the genetics are all well known, understood and documented," I continued, "which pretty much negates consideration of human birth as a miracle."

"So, what do you consider a miracle to be? Do you consider yourself to be nothing more than water, chemicals and proteins mixed together at the proper ratios and temperatures, for a time sufficient to result in the creation of an embryo that grows into a human being? Is a baby nothing more than a fresh baked cake?"

"Well, it's more complex than just that," I offered defensively. "But biologically, we *are* animals."

"Indeed, it is much more complex than that and much different from even the most complex animals," Mom replied. "The creation of a human life is so much, much more than simply chemistry and biology." I looked at her without comment. She continued: "It is more because human beings are more—they are imbued with so much more of the Creator's essence than are animals. This essence is what people refer to as spirit and it is truly divine in its nature. People are God-like in their spirituality because they share God's spirit. This is why in the scriptures, it states that we were created in God's image and given domain over the animals. Human life is divine in nature because every human life is imbued with a portion of God. It is, therefore, both sacred and divine from the very moment of conception. To abort an unborn child is to deny physical life to a part of God."

We sat in silence, me dwelling upon what she had said, she upon the further explanations she was preparing to offer. "The 'miracle of human birth' *IS* miraculous because, at conception, each of us is imbued with a portion of the spirit of God, the creator. And our portions, as human beings, are so much greater than that allowed to even the most intelligent animals, as to permit us to grasp—even if not understand—the infinity of God. It is this spiritual aspect that separates us from lower animals and makes us in the image of God. It is what gives us domain over the physical world even as we constitute, individually, an infinitesimally small part of it.

But remember," Mom continued, "that this spirit is a part of us from the moment we are conceived as humans and existed even *before* that moment. This is why the abortion of a fetus is no different than the taking of *any* human life on a *spiritual* level. The spiritual divinity of human life is sacred. And only those who deny their own spiritual connection to God can justify ending the life of an unborn fetus."

I contemplated what she had said. The logic was simple yet irrefutable. Human life *was* sacred, made so by our inborn spiritual connection to God. To think otherwise was to ignore that with which every culture ever existent had tried to connect. Those who fancied themselves to be atheists did so by dwelling solely upon the physical world to the exclusion of all that preceded or followed it. Somehow, I was beginning to understand. Somehow, I was beginning to grasp the nature and the magnitude of the *spirit*—of the miracle if you will.

"Mom, I think I understand."

"No," she said immediately, "you don't. The first step in understanding is to recognize how much you *don't* know. You are still possessed by the human arrogance that you know all you need. Thinking that, cuts you off from the spiritual basis that all of us share and dooms you, after your physical existence is ended, to an existence as a non-entity; possessed of fleeting thoughts and a sense of self-awareness but without any connection that would provide a true existence."

I looked at her, a shocked expression on my face. I tried to disarm her with humor. "Well," I said, "that certainly puts the fear of the Lord in me."

"It certainly should. Unfortunately, your arrogance condemns you to suffer before you can fully understand."

More than disappointed, I was shattered by her rejection of what I considered to be a personal epiphany on my part. In dejection, I turned my back to her to contemplate my situation.

Understanding my thinking she spoke again: "There is no such thing as a *personal* epiphany. To be one with God requires accepting the uniting of one's existence with His grand design; recognizing oneself as merely a part of the whole; becoming an extension of God rather than a separate being who acknowledges Him."

I turned back towards her for additional explanation. Again, she was gone. Again, I awaited my descent into total deprivation. Only this time, I didn't find myself dematerializing into non-existence. Rather, I found myself pondering what she had just said. My thoughts continued from what she had told me. She had given me a foundation upon which my further thoughts could be built. For the first time, a session of serious consideration did not conclude with me drifting back into the void.

Chapter 12
EXTERNAL FORGIVENESS

My vacuous existence, however, was not yet fully behind me.

It occurred, this time, like the movement of a clock's hour hand; so gradual as to be imperceptible even though its progress was continuous. The lucidity of my thoughts was gradually diminished; the continuity giving way to rambling; the rambling disintegrating to disconnected scraps of unrelated content; the content evaporating. My only awareness was of self…and the overwhelming nothingness in which I dwelt; the deafening roar of silence, the crush of nothing, glimmers of light which revealed no sights. But this time, I realized, a greater part of my awareness remained affording me at least the liberty of contemplation. My thinking continued, and I was increasingly aware of *it*, even if nothing else.

It was, I considered, becoming easier to connect my being with my experiences. I had progressed in my attempts to reconstruct memories and experiences and could form them into *new* thoughts. I found this to be amusing in some perverse way; so much so that I could not stifle a laugh.

I was at Mom's cousin Ted's cabin at Lemon Lake in Southern Indiana. Mom and Dad, my sister and Jerry, Ted and her husband Mac, their kids Sue and Ronnie, my grandma and grandpa, all were there for a cookout. Mom and I sat alone by the edge of the pond, holding cane poles, the hooks baited with grubs, with which we pulled up occasional bluegills. "What's so funny?" Mom asked.

"I don't know," I replied. "I was just thinking."

"That's a very good sign. Having the peace of mind and the solitude to just think is a blessing. It allows you to get closer to God. That's what happens when one meditates…or fishes," she added with a chuckle. She didn't bother to ask of *what* I was thinking—she probably knew anyway. "Do you find yourself *just thinking* more often, recently?"

She *DID* know. She knew what I was thinking. Why else would she have asked that question? "Yes," I replied simply.

She leaned over, placed her arms around me and gave me a hug. "Good. Then *my* prayers are answered. You *are* getting closer."

"To what?"

"To God. Do you fear God?"

"In a Biblical sense or practically speaking?"

This time *she* laughed. "What do you think is the difference?"

"Well, in the Bible we're told to love God and also to fear him. If you love God, I would think there is no need to be afraid of him. I would like to think that I love him and, therefore, don't need to fear him."

"Perhaps," Mom replied. "But if you don't love him, then you *better* be afraid of him. Let me ask you a direct question: do you love the void?"

"I hate it. I'm terrified of it. It's hell isn't it?"

She again chose to ignore this question. "Do you know why you've experienced it?"

I thought before replying. "Because I'm not fully with God," I offered.

"To be fully with God," she continued without pause, acknowledging (I assumed) the correctness of my answer, "is to be totally at peace. Are you totally at peace with yourself?"

"I know I did a lot of things that I regretted. Some were things I did to others. Some were things I did to myself. Some of them caused hurt. Some were violations of what you and Dad had taught me and what was in the Bible. But I truly believe that I asked for God's forgiveness and was forgiven."

"And for those things you *were* forgiven. And the peace you received as a result allows you to now be closer to God than you might otherwise be."

I turned away to consider what she had just said. "Then why did I experience the void? What is preventing me from being with God fully?"

"Look within your heart," she said. "Forgiveness is not just something you get. It is also—maybe even more importantly—something you *give*. Most of all, look to Jesus Christ for example. Even as he was approaching death upon the cross, what did he do?" Strangely, her voice sounded distant and hollow like an echo in a cavern.

"He forgave those who were about to kill him," I replied, even as I contemplated my own answer.

I turned toward the direction of her voice. I saw only the dimness from which it had come.

The dimness darkened.

Chapter 13

THE BRIDGE

Having no concept of time, I'd no idea of how long I had been back in the void. But it seemed the lucidity of my thoughts hadn't really ended. My thoughts had simply paled as if I hadn't really reentered the void but instead was in a late twilight or very early dawn.

I sensed his presence even before the darkness abated. It was as if I stood at the side of a country road at night and sensed a putrefied beagle's rotting body even before I identified its stench or laid eyes upon its mangled form. Obtaining a semblance of physical form, I turned to see *him* looking at me, that same detestable half sneer on his curled partial lips, remnants of his brain still spilling over the bone shards that remained of his destroyed cranium.

Ignoring the visual distress caused me by the long-ago bullet's exit wound, I resolved not to allow my revulsion to force me back to the void.

"Why is it," he asked, a restrained smile replacing his sneer, "that we seem doomed to keep encountering one another like this throughout eternity?"

"Frankly, I can't think of anything I ever did to deserve this; or *you*," I added. I emphasized "you" as if he were a curse. "And I know that of those things I *did* do that were wrong, I've been forgiven."

He turned his back to me, even as he began speaking:

"Remember," he began, "when in church the vicar would say *peace be with you,* and you would reply *and also with you?* Did you ever ask yourself why *peace* had such a prominent place in the liturgy? Did you ever question what it really was or why it was essential?"

I would not patronize him; I would not dignify his question with a reply (although somehow his question intrigued me). He continued, oblivious to my lack of answer. "Peace," he continued, "cannot be one-sided. It is something that must be shared by all who are in conflict with one another or it cannot exist. There can be no peace when even one being feels hate for another. Do you know where you are?"

"Hell obviously," I replied. "You're here, after all."

He smiled. "As are you," he said simply and knowingly, pausing for effect. "You know," he continued, "what separates heaven from hell?"

I chose, again, not to reply. *Your presence,* I thought to myself.

"Peace," he replied simply, in answer to his own question. "One cannot be in heaven without being at peace. And one cannot be at peace with oneself when one is not at peace with another. To be with the creator, one must be at peace. To not be at peace…" his voice trailed off, leaving it to me to draw my own conclusion.

"One can't be at peace when one hates," Billy continued. He nodded at me as if to accuse me of being a hater, "or if one is hated," he added, lowering his hands, palms forward, as he dropped his head like a guilty child. "Our time on Earth," he continued, "truly *is* a test. If we leave it being *hated* because of what we have done, or if we leave it *hating* because of what others have done, we cannot be at peace. And if we cannot be at peace, we cannot be with God. And if we cannot be with God, there is only one alternative."

"Frankly," I said, "I find it sickeningly ironic to have *you*—of all beings—lecturing *me* about salvation. It's rather like sharing communion with the devil."

I glanced at him to gauge his reaction to my words.

There was none.

He wasn't there.

Nothing was.

All that remained were my thoughts...splintered as they were.

Then came the void. Again.

Chapter 14

RESOLUTION

Alone again in the terrifying, sterile, stultifying monotony of the void, I tried to lash on to anything that would lift me from it.

I tried to think of the spirit of my mother. But my thoughts were evanescent like a lone raindrop on a hot summer sidewalk: impact, visible momentary wetness, then gone without a trace. I tried to think of my father but the task was beyond my almost nonexistent powers of concentration.

No matter what I attempted to picture in my thinking, it simply evaporated before it could take shape. With one exception: the one exception I fought to *remove* from my thoughts was seared into them irreparably: my niece's husband, Billy.

No matter what I attempted to picture in my thoughts, it was immediately obfuscated then replaced by the image of him, his skull hanging open and his brain spilling out, a sneer upon his lips, my niece dead upon the carpet, my sister's body lying next to her, desperately clinging to the few remnants of life contained within it.

I was with him again. I couldn't fight it. I couldn't remove myself. I couldn't think of anything else. There was nothing else; just me and the person I hated. I glared at him. Only this time, he didn't appear to me as the sneering apparition I'd encountered before. He turned to hide the gaping hole in his skull and his missing eye from me. He lowered his chin to his shoulder as he turned his remaining eye in my direction, thereby hiding the grotesque deformities left by the bullet as it had entered his jaw and exited his brain.

From this perspective, he didn't look like the monster I reviled. He looked, instead, quite normal. And rather than the sneer that I hated, he wore on his face a look of sympathy and perhaps even serenity.

"Why?" was all I could say.

He fought long and hard in his consideration before replying. "As I said before: human conflict. There truly are only four resolutions to it: murder, suicide, apology or forgiveness."

"But most conflicts are resolved far short of murder…or suicide…" I observed.

"Yes, by apology or forgiveness. And usually, they are inseparable. One party forgives and the other apologizes. One party apologizes and the other forgives. One resolution precedes and the other follows; this is the way it is with resolutions. In our cases, neither of us was willing to take the first step. The conflict grew and festered like an open wound until…" His voice trailed off.

"This is bullshit," I yelled. "You're just looking to share the blame for your monstrous acts by making her responsible for the conflict."

"We were both responsible because neither of us provided an acceptable resolution," he said judiciously. "I think you might be somewhat placated to know that she and I found peace with one another in the afterlife. Even as I was committing the unthinkable act against her, even when I tried to commit the same act against your sister, even as I was committing the unforgivable act against myself, I was begging her and your sister for their forgiveness and God for His. And they in their own sweet ways, found it in their souls to forgive me. As did the creator," he continued.

Even without the physical capacity to produce tears, I knew well the angst and wrenching emotions I felt: I was crying. I wanted to believe him. I wanted to give him the benefit of the doubts I harbored. But he was a charlatan, practiced at turning others to his perverse ways of thinking. I couldn't stand to face him. I turned away from him, my eyes downcast. I had been here so often before. I knew what was coming. I would lift my head and open my eyes to nothing. I would again be returned to the void, insulated from anything and everything I had ever loved, condemned to an eternity of non-existence.

With considerable resolve, I raised my head and opened my eyes, anticipating the nothingness that would be revealed. But instead...

She looked at me and I looked at her without speaking. She was that same, beautiful, glowing, radiant young woman I had watched grow to adulthood. I was dumbstruck. She spoke first: "Hi Uncle Steve. I am happy you've made it this far."

We embraced. Dawn kissed me upon my cheek. Almost instinctively, I turned my head to look for him. He was not there. Nothing was...just a void. I stifled a scream and turned back in Dawn's direction, relieved to find her still standing there, still smiling.

"Why..." I started to question. But she cut me off, beginning to answer my un-asked question.

"He and you are relegated to the void," Dawn began, "by hate. The hate you feel *for* your memories of him and the hate he receives *from* your memories of him, condemns you both.

As I lay on the floor dying," she continued, "at first I felt uncontrollable anger; anger that he was taking me away from my life; anger that he was taking me away from our son; jealousy that he would have him all to himself; rage over what he did to Mom. But as I got closer and closer to passing, that anger began to change. It changed to sympathy for him for the distress he had endured and was enduring. Then pity for him because I knew his soul would not find peace. Even as the last traces of physical life were draining from my body, I was praying to God knowing I would soon be dead. I prayed first for our baby son; that he would have a good and happy life. I prayed for Mom and Dad, for Scott, for my Grandmas and Grandpa, for you and for all my family to have the strength to deal with the hurt and sorrow my passing would cause. And with my last thoughts before I passed, I prayed for him. I prayed that he would be forgiven for what he had done and that he, in time, would find eternal peace. And as I passed, I prayed I would be forgiven for not reconciling our differences earlier. At the instant of my passing, I forgave him and begged God's forgiveness of me."

Overpowered by her words, I again turned from her, only to find myself gazing once more into the void. Frightened by it, I abruptly returned to her. But she wasn't there. But neither was the void.

He was. But this time, I found myself looking into *both* of his blue eyes. His horrific, deforming wounds were not there. Dawn's words dwelt in my thoughts as, for the first time I considered the trials and anguish *he* must have endured.

He didn't speak. He just stood there gazing at me, an almost serene expression on his face.

I extended my hand. He took it in his with a firm grasp. "Peace be with you," I said.

"And also with you," he replied.

Letting go of one another's hands, we embraced.

We separated, I turned and found myself praying:

> *Dear God, forgive me for my sins. Forgive me for the hate I have harbored. Forgive Billy for his sins. Please God, let us find peace with one another and with ourselves.*
>
> *In Jesus Christ's name, I pray.*
>
> *Amen.*

Chapter 15

REDEMPTION

When I turned away from him, from habit I looked toward the void. Only this time, there was no eternal blankness. Rather, I was blinded by brilliance. The light was completely overwhelming obscuring everything within its aura. Gradually I was able to accommodate the glare and began to make out images.

It was the souls of people; people I knew and had thought of often. I recognized them just as I imagined them. They were all there: Mom, Dad, my sister, Jerry, Sue, my children, grandchildren, grandparents, my first wife, Sue's children, in-laws, aunts, uncles, cousins, friends, teachers, associates and acquaintances—almost everyone I had ever held dear was there. They all seemed happy to see me.

The tightly packed crowd parted and through it a lone figure strode from the distant side, too far away to be recognizable, yet obviously headed directly toward me. Half-way through the gathering, I recognized him. He was holding hands with my niece as he stepped toward me. "Thank you," Billy said as he reached me.

The crowd applauded loudly then went silent.

"And I thank you; both of you, for helping me to understand."

A presence so magnificent as to be indescribable followed the same path Billy and Dawn had taken to me. Within the crowd of those gathered, each head bowed as the presence moved by them. Not by sound, not by words, yet by something recognizable to all, the presence communicated to me and to all gathered, a single concept: "Welcome." I knew with no explanation necessary that I was in the presence of the Creator.

And behind him, another presence followed. Wearing a dazzling white, loose-fitting robe, his long hair framed the radiance that shown from his face. I was awestruck; Jesus looked exactly as I had expected him to look during my life on Earth.

Turning to my right, I found I was standing next to Farid with whom I had worked early on during my during my physical life. I gave him a hug; it had been such a long time since I had seen him. "I just can't believe what I am seeing," I said.

"Yes, my friend," he replied. "It is the Creator, followed by Mohammed." His observation left me perplexed. I had seen Jesus; Farid had seen Mohammed.

A firm hand settled upon my shoulder from behind. "See," my Dad's voice said, "it's just like I said. Seek and ye shall find. But there are corollaries to 'seek and ye shall find'," he continued. "We do find what we seek; and *what* we seek determines *what* we find."

I stood in silence, contemplating the enormous simplicity of my Dad's words.

Movement at my feet caught my attention and my eyes turned downward. Turning three revolutions within his body length, and then sitting down on his haunches, Buddy dropped a saliva-covered tennis ball at my feet then sat there in anticipation of the throw he knew would soon follow.

I bent to pick up the ball. Feeling a slight lump in the pocket of my jeans, I reached in and extracted the gold railroad pocket watch which had been my great grandfather's, passed down to me through three generations. From habit, I flipped open the cover to check the time.

It was 7:35…more or less.

The Beginning

____

Judgement

The good or evil that one does is not weighed upon a balance,
nor comingled in the fog that in time is history,
but rather stands apart, and overwhelms the other,
leaving it alone as one's legacy.

About this book

"*7:35*" began as an effort on my part to provide a "unification theory" of religion, seeking to bundle together my Christian religious upbringing with my secular education and philosophies in a manner to which my adult children could relate. More importantly, I sought to share a spiritual connection between life and Creation with those without one. In short order as it developed, it took on so many characters and situations from my life experience that it became virtually autobiographical, yet where was the connection I'd originally sought?

For me the writing of this book reaffirmed the Christian values I had been taught as a child which have been carried with me (stumbles and deviations notwithstanding) since. More importantly, it attempted to connect them with an infinity so vast as to not be comprehended by the limits of a human existence bounded by limited experience.

Virtually all the situations described—from the fight behind the high school, my mother's counseling of me, my experiences with "Father Flipout," to the murder of my niece and shooting of my sister, and many others—have in fact marked my life.

Excepting family members, names of characters herein have been omitted or changed to protect their identities.

Amongst all the people to whom I am indebted for their support in this effort, at the forefront of the list is my wife Susan and my sister Cheryl; both have endured some of the greatest tragedies which life can bestow (some included and some not included herein) yet both survived them and persevered with their faiths and relationships with the Creator intact.

They, as much as anything else I've experienced, are responsible for what I hope is the joyous message (overall) contained in the text.

I would also like to thank collaborators who had the patience to wade through my rough drafts and manuscripts offering critiques and encouragement; Col. Fred McClintock (USAF, Ret.), Hanne Sweetnam-Boyd (R.I.P.), my first wife Joyce, my son Greg, my daughter Christine, my best friend from childhood Richard J. Carriger, and Reverend Roy Schneider (R.I.P.).

About the author

Steve Percifield, born and raised in Indianapolis, has lived and worked in New York City, St. Louis, Baltimore, Pleasant Lake, MI, Louisville, KY and, since 1983, the Chicago area, currently residing in Joliet, IL.

A graduate of Indiana University, most of his adult life has been spent in business-to-business marketing within the bakery foods industry.

Author of numerous magazine articles and publisher of a bakery trade journal, he has authored two books; one a guide to personal investment strategies, the other *Grease Monkey,* the story (based on real lives) of a bi-racial automobile racing team during the 1910s and 1920s and their confrontations with institutionalized racism and the Ku Klux Klan in Indiana.

In Praise of
"Seven, Thirty-Five"

…Amazing. Everything is written so vividly, I felt I could actually see what was being described. Soon after I started reading it, I found that this had a personal place in your life. Beautifully written. I totally agree that everybody deserves to be forgiven for their sins, so that we may be at peace.
I was captivated throughout the story. I am glad that I had the opportunity to read it.

Jacqueline Ezzell

…very clever how you tied together your family, your spiritual journey, and a touch of Rod Serling to tell this story. …very brave thing to write, particularly because of the tragic nature of some of the personal encounters.

Lew Karp

"Gripping. I couldn't put it down. Very intelligently written."

Rev. Roy Schneider (R.I.P.)